A Complicated Situation

A Complicated Situation

Stories by
JANE MULLEN

SOUTHERN METHODIST
UNIVERSITY PRESS
Dallas

These stories are works of fiction. Names, characters, places, and incidents are either the product of the author's imagination or are used fictitiously.

Requests for permission to reproduce material from this work should be sent to:
Rights and Permissions
Southern Methodist University Press
PO Box 750415
Dallas, Texas 75275-0415

Jacket art: Ron Dale, *The Last Family Heirloom,* 1991, 88" x 46" x 13", low-fire ceramic, polychromed wood. From the collection of Billy and Julie Chadwick.

Jacket and text design: Tom Dawson Graphic Design

LIBRARY OF CONGRESS CATALOGING-IN-PUBLICATION DATA
Mullen, Jane.
        A complicated situation : stories / by Jane Mullen. — 1st ed.
        p.   cm.
        Contents: Deserters — That's no way — Everything goes — Dardis and me — The one with the heart — Taking off — Holly's landing — Still in Mississippi — A complicated situation.
        ISBN 0-87074-431-3 (acid-free paper)
        1. United States—Social life and customs—20th century—Fiction.
I. Title.
PS3563.U39544C66   1998
813'.54—dc21   98-36287

Printed in the United States of America on acid-free paper
10   9   8   7   6   5   4   3   2   1

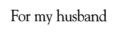

For my husband

ACKNOWLEDGMENTS

These stories were originally published, some in slightly different form, in the following publications: "Dardis and Me" in *Mademoiselle*, "Deserters" and "Holly's Landing" in *Prairie Schooner*, "The One with the Heart" in *Alaska Quarterly Review*, "Everything Goes" in *River Oak Review*, and "Still in Mississippi" in *American Literary Review*. The author is grateful to the Mississippi Arts Commission for its support.

Thanks are also due to Greg Johnson, to my husband Greg Schirmer, to Tom McHaney, David Galef, and Kos Kostmayer, with special thanks to Kathryn Lang and Freddie Jane Goff.

CONTENTS

Deserters

My father spent his weekends, in the coastal corner of New Hampshire where we battled the elements, making a fortress of our house. He weather-stripped windows and doors, added layers of insulation to the attic walls and ceilings, reshingled the roof, scraped, sanded and painted storm windows until they locked snugly into place. He attacked with putty and plaster any crack or pinhole that threatened to let warmth escape, stockpiled candles and firewood against power failures, and stacked the basement shelves with enough canned goods to weather the longest winter storm. Conditioned as he was to sealing us in and the elements out, he was dismayed to read of four children in nearby Portsmouth who died in an early-morning fire, sealed inside a house as snug as ours, and he turned his attention to plotting our escape, installing rope ladders in our bedroom windows and conducting fire drills so that we could practice our getaway in all kinds of weather.

My brother Neil and I became adept at rising from the deepest sleeps to remove screens or storm windows and scramble down our perilously swinging ladders. Then we would dash barefoot to the triple oak tree designated as our meeting place for a head count. My mother took no part in the fire drills and regarded them with amusement. Taking our cue from her, Neil and I thought of them as a kind of game, especially after they were relegated to the daytime hours when all the neighborhood kids would gather in our yard to cheer us on and time our escapes. We knew they envied us our rope ladders, and our father, so we didn't really mind being made conspicuous.

Generally we took my father's precautions for granted, until he slipped from the wet roof, where he had climbed to replace some shingles torn loose by Hurricane Helen, and fell to his death. He had provided against that event too, with an insurance policy that paid the mortgage on the house and a doubly generous reward for accidents. But my father's death left us exposed in ways he could not have foreseen and our sorrow was sharpened by a fine edge of resentment at his desertion.

I was nine and for the first time afraid. My room was on the side of the house that faced a field where in summer the grass grew taller than I was. Beyond the field was a woods, and beyond the woods, standing next to the town library, was the county jail, from which prisoners had been known to escape. Shortly before my father died, a policeman had rapped on our door at dawn and told us to stay inside and keep the house locked, and we'd all stood together in our bathrobes at my bedroom window as a phalanx of policemen, guns drawn, were dragged through the field and into the woods by a pack of ferociously sniffing dogs. I wasn't at all afraid then. But now, nightly, I saw escaped prisoners quietly removing screens and storm windows, climbing in without a sound, moving through the house on silent feet. If I slept facing the open door of my room I was afraid I would see them creeping up the stairs and down the hall. If I slept with my back to the door I was afraid of being stabbed in the back. If I shut the door I was afraid of being the last to know about the fire that was sure to break out in the kitchen. No matter how I slept, I had nightmares. I would wake myself up with the screams that shrieked in my own ears but that Neil, when he heard them across the hall, said came out like the tiny squeals of a trapped mouse. My mother, who slept with the aid of tranquilizers now, never surfaced before morning.

WHEN THE FIRST WAVE of her grief subsided, my mother smiled at Neil across the kitchen table one Saturday morning. "You're the man of the family now."

"No," he said right away, as if he'd been expecting those exact words. "I'm only eleven years old."

Surprised, my mother looked at him, then at me. But I looked away. No one said anything for a long time. "Then we'll take in boarders," my mother said, suddenly putting down her coffee cup. Neil looked bewildered, puzzled, I suppose, by the "then," but I was immediately entranced by the idea of permanently occupied guest rooms and populous, noisy meals.

After taking a survey of the second floor my mother, who had a distaste for strangers, decided to rent only one room on the third floor, where there was a separate bathroom. She hung fresh curtains on the double sets of casement windows, brought up the best sheets and guest towels from the linen cupboard, called in a man to resurface the pitted, claw-footed bathtub, put an ad in the newspaper, and ordered Neil and me to remove all our belongings from the third-floor playroom, because we would not be allowed to go up there anymore.

So began the long line of men who quietly let themselves in through the front door and crept up the stairs to the third floor. They were not really boarders, because they were given no meals. Nor were they allowed to use the kitchen or to keep food in their room. All that was wanted was a trustworthy man to sleep under our roof at night. For the rest they were expected to make themselves invisible. There were to be no late hours, no guests, no lingering outside the house, even on the hottest of summer days.

The actual presence of these men in our house seemed to offend more than reassure my mother. Beyond the first interview she had no dealings with them. She never greeted them when they came in or went out, and they soon learned not to speak to her either. None of them could figure out which door to use, and I think my mother couldn't decide either which was a greater invasion of privacy, their walking the length of the living room when she was reading there and going up the front stairs, or coming through the kitchen on their way to the back stairs. The more sensitive ones tried to guess which part of the house she was in and would walk around to the other side. They all tried to pay her at first, until they devised their various ways of leaving envelopes, on their dresser, on the hall table, the kitchen table. One roomer used to leave it on the floor outside her bedroom door, which she particularly disliked.

For the first two years, none of them stayed long, naturally. They either left in a few weeks for more hospitable quarters, or they were asked to leave: Mr. Stillman because he kept boxes of muffins under the bed, Mr. Bellows because he hung objectionable calendars on the wall, Mr. Hanley because he often tossed a handful of Tootsie Rolls on my bed when he passed my open door. I missed all of them when they left, until Norman, the last of our protectors, moved in and the rest of them faded into a long gray line of dreary men in business suits.

Even Norman's initial interview was different. It lasted much longer than any of the others had, and when he left my mother didn't have that bruised look she always wore after those encounters. Hopping from foot to foot, impatient for her verdict, I watched from the doorway, already in love. "Are we taking him?"

"I don't understand," she said, "why a man like that is working in a factory. It doesn't make any sense." But I knew she was going to take him even before she sent me for the ammonia and paper towels. "We'll go up and give those windows a polish," she said. "And bring another pillow from the linen closet. He probably likes to read in bed."

That Saturday, when Norman pulled up in his white Studebaker, Neil and I were sitting on the front steps with my friend Carrie Gilbert, waiting for him. I'd told Carrie she could stay just long enough to get a look. "My God," she whispered, as he came up the walk. "He looks just like Buddy Holly." When he smiled at us, a smile that ended up being all the more a smile for its starting out like a slice of pain, I saw she was right. He shook hands with Neil and said he could use some help.

I had to warn Carrie off with a look. She sulked away in the direction of her house while Neil and I elbowed each other. None of the other roomers had ever brought more than a suitcase or two, but Norman's car was packed to the roof with duffel bags and boxes. He had a radio, a typewriter, a gooseneck desk lamp, a rolled exercise mat, a set of barbells Neil made a grab for but couldn't budge, and an electric percolator. Neil and I exchanged a look over the percolator, but didn't say anything.

As the weeks passed without a word from my mother about the aroma of coffee drifting down the stairs, or the bags from Pacelli's bakery that were carried up, it became clear that Norman was going to be allowed to break all the rules, and I resolved to watch him carefully, to see how it was done. But for a long time I didn't see much of him. He worked the evening shift and came in long after I was asleep. Yet in the morning when I woke up I could hear his typewriter already going. My mother said he kept at it all day, except on cleaning days, when he went out, she had no idea where. She didn't think he ever slept; she seemed pleased by the idea.

I STILL HAD NIGHTMARES. One night I dreamt I was in the house alone, walking from room to room, checking the doors and windows. In the kitchen I found the door to the cellar wide open, although I knew I'd locked it. I pushed it shut and leaned against it with my shoulder and tried to lock it again. But someone much stronger pushed against it from the other side, and I knew it was my father, trying to get in.

Norman's hand gripped my shoulder, waking me. "I was just coming in. I heard you. I've heard you before. Do you want your mother?" I pushed my face into the pillow and heard him knocking on her door. After a few minutes, he came back. "You'd better go yourself," he said. "She didn't answer."

"She takes pills."

"Ah," he said. "Well, do you want me to turn your light on?" I shook my head and waited for him to go away, but he stood there. After a minute I felt him sit on the edge of the bed. I felt him smile.

"What are you so afraid of?"

"Everything."

"Everything! You're not afraid of me, are you?" He didn't wait for an answer. He asked if I was afraid of other things, stupid things, like answering the telephone and going to school. I kept shaking my head, no.

"Then what *are* you afraid of?"

I rolled over and looked at him. "Fire. Murderers. Air raid drills. Ghosts."

"Air raid drills I can understand," he said. "But ghosts? How old are you?"

That put me on the defensive. I told him about my dream, and about other dreams. I told him about my father and the fire drills and the escaped prisoner, and how I couldn't bring myself to go into the woods anymore. It was easy to talk to him because he wasn't really looking at me. He sat sideways and listened with his profile, like a priest listening to your confession.

"You're not afraid of everything," he said. "You're afraid of one thing. You're afraid of dying." He softened the accusation by saying that under the circumstances it was only natural. He didn't say anything else for a while. Then he asked me if I was reading Shakespeare yet.

"We did *Midsummer Night's Dream.*"

"Look at *Julius Caesar* sometime," he said. "It's certainly not the best play, but there's a line there that I've had time and reason to think about a lot. The gist of it is that a brave man dies only once. But a coward dies a thousand times." He touched my cheek with the back of his hand and got up. "That goes for women too, of course."

"Norman?" I didn't want him to go. "Do you think I'm a coward?" What I really wanted to say was, Do you really think I'm a woman?

"Not yet," he said, and shut the door.

A FEW WEEKS LATER, I discovered where Norman spent cleaning days. We had just finished reading "Evangeline" and had to write a paper on it. Carrie and I went to the library after school. We didn't look for books about Longfellow or about poetry; we had discovered that we could get A's by fleshing out meager essays with photographs and drawings and arranging them in folders. We surrendered our book bags at the desk and went into the art room where we pulled out the file drawer marked "L."

On the way to Longfellow something else caught our eye and we pulled it out. It was a black and white sketch of an army of rats swarming down a bluff and across a wide beach, into the ocean. It was clear that the vanguard of rats was already drowned and those behind them in the process of drowning. Yet none turned back. We stared at it a long time, attracted by the sheer inexplicability of it. The strip of paper stapled beneath said only, "Lemmings march to the sea." I checked out the drawing, along with another of "Evangeline and Gabriel pale with emotion."

On the way out we saw Norman at a table in the corner of the reference room. He had seen us too, so we went over. He was writing on a sheet of yellow paper, and there was a stack of filled pages turned upside down at his elbow. I asked what he was doing.

"Some detective work," he said. "Research."

"What for?"

"For a book."

"Are *you* writing a book?" I had only thought of books as things that were read, not things that were written, certainly not by someone you knew, on ordinary paper with a ball-point pen.

"I might," he said. "If I'm left alone long enough."

I thought he meant us and I started to back off. But Carrie sat down next to him and tried to read what he had written. "Is it a mystery?"

Norman shuffled his papers. You could see he didn't want to tell her, so I took out my drawing of Evangeline and Gabriel and showed it to him. He snorted at it and then read the caption in falsetto. I took it back and put it in my folder. I knew I couldn't use it now.

"Will you drive us home, Norman?" Carrie asked him. "Laura won't cut through the woods. We have to walk all the way around. It'll be dark."

"What do you know about lemmings?" I asked on the way home. I held up my sketch and he glanced at it.

"They're rodents," he said, "who've devised a unique solution to their population problem. They tend to over-copulate. I assume you know what that means. And when their food runs out they set off in armies to search for more. But somewhere along the line they lose sight of their objective. They climb mountains, cross streams, rivers, fields, and when they reach the sea they simply keep going. They swim on until they drown."

"But can't the ones on the bluff see what's happening?" I held up the drawing again. "Can't they see all the ones in front are dead? Don't they ever turn back? Not even one?"

"If one does turn back," Norman said, looking straight ahead, "the other rats go after him."

"But why?"

"Why indeed."

IN NOVEMBER NORMAN GAVE my mother roses. I did know what copulate meant by then because, finding the dictionary no help, I had asked my mother and she had told me. But our talk had not gone well. I had wanted only a simple answer, but she had evidently been looking for an opportunity to unleash a whole Pandora's box of terrors, clumsily and all at once. I was furious with her, and she in turn was irritated with me, and this time our bad tempers didn't evaporate overnight. We brought them to the breakfast table morning after morning until so many weeks passed I was afraid we'd never get back to where we'd been before.

Norman knew it was her birthday because Neil and I had asked him to drive us out to a nursery that had advertised a white wicker garden chair for twenty dollars. Neil had had his eye on a canister set of lacquered wood for four dollars and had pointed out to me that snow was on the ground and that our mother hardly ever sat outside. But we carried our separate visions of her and in mine, which I was desperately trying to recapture, she was dressed in white, ensconced in the white chair, under the white birch trees. In the end, Neil agreed to go halves.

Her birthday was on a Sunday and we found the roses on the hall table when we came in from church. As planned, Norman had brought in the chair from the garage while we were gone and had propped up the card we had signed. My mother walked all around the chair without saying anything, trailing her hand over its high back, before she sat in it, still speechless. Neil handed her the roses. When he laid them in her arms she looked just like a Queen for a Day, tears and all. Then she reached both arms up to bring us within kissing range. When she found her voice she asked if we'd mind asking Norman to join us for dinner.

Neil and I were in the kitchen scraping vegetables when he came down the back stairs, dressed for the occasion. Neil whistled. "Hey, Norman. I didn't know you owned a tie." Norman went to the refrigerator and took out a bottle of champagne he must have put there when we went to church. So we knew he'd expected to be asked. Neil's eyes lit up when he saw the champagne; he told me to get out four wineglasses.

Dinner was more than an hour later than we had planned, because Neil and I were doing the cooking and we had a lot of trouble synchronizing things. But my mother and Norman didn't seem to mind. We could hear them talking the whole time in the living room. Every once in a while we'd hear my mother laugh and we'd look at each other triumphantly, as if we'd done it.

We ate in the dining room for the first time since my father died, and we raided his store of squat candles for the table, thinking to make up in number what they lacked in height. My mother brought her new chair to the table and sat in it. It was a garden chair, far too low for the table, and she had trouble seeing Norman through the candles and roses. I can still see her inclining her head from side to side, smiling, her eyes bright. She was only thirty-six that day, and although it no longer surprises me that she should have been so lovely then, or that a lonely woman should blossom in the presence of a sympathetic man, at the time I was astonished. She seemed to be growing younger before my eyes.

Norman brought out a second bottle of champagne to have with the cake, and we sat around the table sipping it until it was finished. Every time Neil reached for the bottle he would glance at my mother, but she never told him to stop, not even when he spilled some on the tablecloth. He and I were mere spectators, and she was as little distracted by our behavior as an actress by a distant cough in the audience. We did, however, often enter into her conversation with Norman, as characters in the stories she told him. After a while I began to feel like an old photograph, picked up, commented on, discarded.

"Laura," she said towards the end of the meal, after telling Norman how I had cut up some blue velvet dress material to cover the seat of my bicycle, "is exactly like her father. Exactly. But Neil takes after me." Her eyes found Neil, at last, and she smiled at him. I willed her to look at me too, but she wouldn't, and I was horrified to see the candle flames start swimming backstrokes. Norman looked at me, and then at her.

"Laura has your eyes," he said. "And your hair."

"My hair?" She reached up quickly and touched it, as if I might have taken it from her.

Neil was violently sick after dinner. My mother took him upstairs and Norman took off his coat, rolled up his sleeves, and helped me with the dishes. We worked in silence for the most part, handling the dishes as if they were much more fragile than they were. Once, Norman asked me what was the matter, but I denied anything was. When we'd finished he took the dish towel from me and spread it to dry.

"I'm going for a walk," he said. "Want to come?" Before I could answer, he added, "I'll tell you a secret. Today is my birthday too." Having nothing else to give him, I put my arms around his waist and gave him a hug.

"How old are you, Norman?"

"Too old for you," he said. "Unhand me now, and get your

coat. Ask your mother first." But I shook my head, and he didn't insist.

"I guess it will be all right," he said.

I wondered why he hadn't gotten any birthday cards, which made me realize he'd never gotten any mail of any kind, not that I knew of, and on our walk I asked him if he had any family.

"I have a sister," he said after a long silence. "Very, very pretty. I never thought much about the way she looked, but other people said she was pretty. When she got to be about your age, more and more people started saying it."

"What did she look like?" I tried to imagine an eleven-year-old female Buddy Holly who was somehow beautiful.

"She looked just like my mother."

"What did *she* look like?"

"She looked just like a painting we had hanging in the dining room. At least that's what our insurance agent used to say. He came once a year to collect the premiums on the different policies, always on my sister's birthday because they'd all been taken out when she was born. His name was Mr. McCormick and he became sort of a friend over the years. My mother always had coffee ready for him, and he usually had a piece of birthday cake, and he *always* mentioned how like that painting my mother was. 'Pure Renoir,' he would say.

"She pretended not to believe a word of it. But I think now that that's why we had that painting. And I think she looked forward to having that said to her every year. I think, in a way, she counted on it. But one year he didn't say it to her. He said it to my sister instead. My sister blushed. Even I could see how pretty she was. My mother tried not to mind. But she did. She couldn't help minding."

"What did she do?"

"She didn't *do* anything. But there was something in the way she looked at my sister that was slightly different after that.

You know the story of Snow White. Mirror, mirror, on the wall. It's a raw deal for the queen after all those years of being the fairest."

I thought of Norman not getting any birthday presents, or cards, or letters. "Was your mother— Well, was she—*evil?*"

He laughed out loud. "No more than yours is."

"Mine?"

"Yours," he said, and touched my hair.

I sifted through his words several times, afraid of missing something, of misunderstanding. But each time I sifted I came up with the same nugget of pure gold. It was a gift, unnecessary and extravagant, and I carried it the rest of the way home wrapped carefully in silence.

IT WAS AFTER NEW YEAR'S that Norman became a full-fledged boarder. There was a blizzard that prolonged our Christmas vacation. Even the ball-bearings factory where Norman worked evenings was shut down. He didn't venture downstairs at all that night, but the next morning my mother opened the door to the third-floor stairs and called up that breakfast was ready. He came down for lunch too, and for dinner. After dinner my mother told him that he shouldn't feel obligated to go back up to his room, unless he wanted to.

After a number of false starts at a number of card games, Norman taught Neil and me how to play poker. We had set up a table in front of the fire and we played for hours. I hoped it would never stop snowing. My mother tried to read at first, but she was too restless. She kept getting up to look out the windows, first one and then another. When she said she thought she'd go up to bed Norman got up and steered her to the card table. We taught her how to play five-card draw, because it was easiest. But she seemed to have an inordinate amount of trouble remembering which was higher than what, and we all knew that deep down she believed a lady shouldn't be able to learn how to play poker. Norman helped her the first few times, looking at her cards and patiently explaining which ones to hold, which to discard, when to bet, when to fold. After a few rounds of the first real game, she looked up, perplexed.

"I forget. Which is better, a straight or a full house?" We all threw down our cards, and she laughed. "Bluff! I don't have a thing."

"You can't do that," Neil said. He appealed to Norman. "Can she do that?"

"I'm afraid she can," Norman said, and you could tell he didn't just mean poker.

I don't know how it was decided that Norman should continue taking all of his meals with us. I never heard it discussed, but it began that night of the blizzard. He continued to sit in my father's chair in the kitchen, and once the cover of snow was lifted we all felt a little exposed, unsure of our roles.

It didn't take Neil and me very long to learn how to turn that uncertainty to our advantage. We saved up all of our bad news for the dinner table, using Norman's presence as a shield. My mother would be forced to say something, and having once responded to us with restraint, could hardly work herself into a fury later. She knew what we were doing. She resented it, and the night Neil announced that he wanted to be a priest, that he was going to the seminary next year instead of the high school, she looked at him with something very like hatred. I was watching, because I knew he was going to tell her. He'd already told me, and I felt like a traitor too, when she said—in a voice that strove for lightness and failed, a voice that walked a tightrope and slipped—"So. You'll desert me? So soon?"

Neil escaped the table early that night, saying he had to go to Louis Tubert's to work on their debate. When he was gone

Norman said he didn't have to go to work that night. He asked us to go to a movie with him, and sent me for the newspaper to see what was playing. As the door between the kitchen and dining room swung shut behind me, I heard him, for the first time, call my mother by her name. "Ellen," he said quietly. "Ellen."

Carrie Gilbert's mother was at *Gigi* that night too. She passed us without a word, but I didn't care. I was transported. I would grow up as suddenly as Gigi. Norman, who thought he was too old for me, would be as dazzled and devoted as Gaston. It was Norman who'd invented champagne.

I HOPED THERE WOULD be roses for my birthday too, and dropped large hints as April rolled around. But I celebrated my twelfth birthday with six girls from my class, and there were no roses or champagne. I didn't even find Norman's present until I went up to bed that night. My room was filled with bright-colored balloons and there was a flat box from the army/navy surplus store on my bed. Inside was an oversized canvas knapsack. I couldn't envision a use for it, but I left my door open and my light on and tried to stay awake to thank him.

When my alarm went off in the morning, the door was shut and the light off. The floor was littered with dead balloons, and I could hear Norman's typewriter going. Before I left for school I packed my books into the knapsack. Backpacks for school would not be in use for years, and I felt pretty daring as I strapped it on.

"Good Lord!" my mother said. "You look like a hobo." But I wore it anyway. Outside, I threw last year's acorns up at Norman's windows until one connected and he looked out. I spun around so he could see the knapsack. He laughed and turned both thumbs up.

Carrie was trying to catch up with Neil when I caught up with her. She didn't even notice my knapsack. She looked after Neil regretfully. "What a waste," she said. "My mother says it's because of Norman, that he has to get away." I just looked at her.

"Are they going to get married?" she said, after a silence.

"Who?" I said.

"Your mother and Norman."

"No," I said. "Why should they?"

Her reply mystified me, because I heard "roomers" instead of "rumors," and didn't get it until halfway through math class. Then scenes started going through my head, backwards, turning everything around. That afternoon I lingered at my locker to give Carrie a good head start before I went home.

When I let myself in through the front door, my mother was just coming down the stairs. She was walking at an uncharacteristic angle and holding on to the banister. Something else was different about her too, a kind of vacancy. Her voice was full of static, like a long-distance operator's.

"Do you know where Norman is?"

"Why?" I asked, jealous. But of him or of her I couldn't say.

She went to the sofa and sat down and started adjusting magazines on the coffee table. I could see her trying to decide whether to tell me or not, and then deciding to, so I waited. She patted the sofa and I sat down next to her. We both perched on the edge, tentatively, temporarily, like people who meet at a party and know right away they won't have much to say to each other. She took her time.

"Norman," her voice shorted out on the word, "is not what he seems, Laura. Even his name is, is something else."

She stopped then to let her words sink in, and my mind was busy with the scene in which he told her. He took the dish towel from her and hung it up to dry. He put his hands on her shoulders. He smiled. I'm not what I seem to be. My real name is—is Buddy Holly.

"His foreman called here a little while ago," she went on. "Some men were at the factory looking for him. They were FBI agents. They're on their way here. He wanted to warn me."

"But why?" I whispered.

"He's a deserter, Laura." I didn't understand.

"You mean he already has a family?" My voice was a wail now.

"A family? What are you talking about? He's a deserter, from the army, from Korea."

"Korea!" I couldn't believe my ears. "We just read about Korea in history."

"There are some things you can never put behind you, Laura. It's not a matter of time." When she looked at me, I saw what was different about her. She had retreated back into mourning, beyond reach.

In my room I emptied my knapsack. I put my books on my desk and worked at getting their spines flush. I lined up my pens and pencils according to size, then color, then size again, as if their arrangement was important. I gathered up all the dead balloons and put them in the bottom drawer. I would never throw them away. Then I went up to Norman's room. I walked around opening drawers, in his desk and his dresser. I looked in his closet, as my mother had looked at my father's things when he was dead and no longer entitled to secrets. But I found no secrets. Norman was exactly what he'd seemed to be. And he wasn't dead. He was in the reference room of the library, on the other side of the woods, wanting nothing more than to be left alone.

I went through his drawers again, more quickly this time, taking things out, old letters, stacks of yellow papers, photographs, everything that made him Norman and not somebody else. I piled them into the wastebasket, which my mother had emptied that day, cleaning day. Then I put in some underwear, socks, a sweater, and ran into the bathroom to take everything out of the medicine cabinet I thought he might need. I was in my room transferring everything from the wastebasket to the knapsack when I heard car doors shutting, and then the doorbell. I packed the knapsack and slung it over my shoulder.

On the stairs I met my mother coming up. The man behind her was carrying a hat and looked like all of the other men who had followed her up the stairs to inspect the spare room before Norman moved in. I looked at my mother resentfully. I didn't see how she could lead him to Norman's trail. I was so sure I would have barred the way. She looked back at me, but didn't say anything, nor did the man with her. But the one inside the front door did. He patted my knapsack.

"And where are you off to? Leaving home?"

"To my girlfriend's," I said. "Homework."

"Better do it here today," he said, smirking back on his heels.

I turned around and headed for the kitchen, intent on going out the back way. It wasn't until I saw the man leaning against the refrigerator that I knew real fear for the first time, the fear of being helpless to protect someone you love. Shaking, I went up the back stairs to my room and sat on the bed, listened to the footsteps overhead, the sound of drawers opening and closing. I thought of my father listening to the wind tearing at the roof. And then I remembered my rope ladder and all those speedy escapes.

I inched my window open and lowered the ladder foot by foot. I strapped the knapsack to my back, climbed down, and then raced to the shelter of the uneven grasses and the woods beyond, where I hadn't been since my father died. I think I already knew I couldn't save Norman from anything. But I ran just the same.

That's No Way

Catherine has already heard from friends that Sam is moving to Los Angeles at the end of the month when he calls her at work on a Tuesday morning to say he'll be winding up a very busy week with a Friday morning appointment at the printers near her office.

"Should we have lunch?"

Should they?

But she knows what he means. He is not referring to the fact that she is married and that he once, years ago, was the man she lived with. They have, after all, had lunch together before. Not often, not more than once a year, if you averaged it out: some years not at all; other years three times. But ten lunches over ten years works out to not more than one a year. Hardly a regular occurrence, nothing to trouble the conscience.

No. His "should we" means something else entirely. It means: if she is still angry because he did not show up last time, last April, then maybe they should not have lunch; maybe she needs a little more time. Most of her anger has leaked away over the intervening months, but not having had the opportunity to be expressed, the dregs remain, dark and bitter-tasting. However, as she has already heard that he will be moving to Los Angeles at the end of the month, and she has some news of her own to give him, too, she says yes, they should have lunch.

On Friday there is a cool breeze, unusual for D.C. in late July. During the night a cold front moving down from somewhere has suddenly kicked off with both feet the oppressive blanket of moist heat that has smothered the city all summer. Sam, with an unusually brown hand, even for him, even for July, indicates the cerulean sky. "This could be anywhere. Maine, Minnesota, October."

Catherine is wearing a hat, a straw hat with a red band and a wide brim the breeze gets under and threatens to lift off. She never used to wear hats, and Sam never used to like changes of any kind, but he gently calms the hat with the flat of his hand and speaks into Catherine's eyes. "Two points for the hat." Catherine waits a minute, to get her voice under control, to pull it up from the bottom of her soul and push it up towards that blue sky like a light, bright balloon. "Are we going to keep score?" She is allowed that much, at least.

Sam is dressed the way he has always dressed; jeans and a khaki workshirt with the sleeves turned back twice. He never changes. "You never change," she says. "You haven't even changed your shirt."

"It's easier this way." He smiles. "It's easier to have only one shirt."

Catherine knows that he now owns dozens of those shirts and that he buys them at Britches in Georgetown. He works for a computer time-sharing company and makes a lot of money. But he used to be poor. He used to teach high school Latin and really did have only one shirt, or so few that he often had to wash one out in the sink at night. In the morning, the shirt would have to be ironed. If Catherine ironed the shirt while he shaved, he would drive her all the way to work. If he had to iron the shirt himself, a process that took him three times longer than it did her, he would drop her at Union Station to catch the bus. She hated ironing cotton shirts; nor did she like being the only white person on the bus. Sam hated ironing, too, and refused to get out of bed the necessary ten minutes earlier. At the time it seemed something of an irreconcilable difference. Now Catherine knows what the phrase really means.

The restaurant is a new Basque place that has only recently opened up and they decide to sit outside in front, their table situated right on the corner of one of Connecticut Avenue's busier intersections. They sit there not only because of the weather, but because they generally like to be out in the open where anyone walking by can see them. See? Nothing wrong here, nothing to hide. No dark boothy bars, no out-of-the-way corners with concealing spider plants. Just old friends having lunch together out here in the open under these bright yellow-and-white striped umbrellas, hundreds of people walking by, cars passing.

But after their first exchange out on the sidewalk, they have trouble getting started. The missed lunch in April hangs heavily, a sword ready to fall, a cloud threatening to open up and cause a rain delay on this beautiful ball-park day. Or maybe it's just that he's moving to Los Angeles at the end of the month and hasn't told her yet. They contemplate their menus in silence, while around them everyone is talking, talking more loudly than they would be if they were inside the restaurant. The two women in dark suits at the next table sound drunk already. At least one of them does, her voice full of shrill emphasis. "I've been upset for three *years* and he doesn't *know* I'm upset. You're upset for three *minutes* and he wants to know how come you're so up*set*. You don't know how *lucky* you are. That's *your* problem."

Catherine and Sam both smile, although not at each other. Then he touches the back of her hand with the back of his and firmly catches her eye, his glance saying: Aren't you glad you're not upset? See what it looks like? See how it sounds? Oh, how well she knows him. And what is she to do with it all, this knowledge, she would like to know? She would like to take it and throw it in the Potomac. But she is stuck with it.

His eyes move back to the menu. "Hmmmm. What shall I drink?"

"Hemlock."

He raises an eyebrow, but says only, "What are you having, Cat? Have something marvelous. Have a lobster. Have a crab."

His voice is contralto and controlled, always heard, never overheard. A civil, civilized voice with just a grain of gravel in it. His voice always reminds Catherine of some powerful thoroughbred, reined in, walking beautifully, deliberately. It was his voice she fell for first, all those years ago.

"Why so extravagant today? You always said lunch was not an occasion, it was just something you did in the middle of the day to keep from getting hungry." She waits for him to tell her that the occasion is he's moving to Los Angeles at the end of the month and this is their last lunch.

"That was a quote," he says. "I stole it from somewhere. Besides, that was when we were living together. We didn't have to meet for lunch."

"And when half your salary was going to your analyst and you couldn't afford to eat lunch."

Catherine still blames the analyst. After Sam quit teaching to go back to Chicago for a degree in computer science and did not ask her to go with him, she used to lie awake at night imagining conversations he might have had with the man he always referred to as "the man."

She wants me to say that I love her. She has to hear me say it.

And do you love her?

That's not the point. She's trying to force my hand. She wants me to make a decision I'm not ready to make.

Perhaps you have already made your decision.

THEY ORDER RUM AND tonics in honor of Sam's past three months in the Bahamas. They never used to drink at lunch. He has always disliked it, and she was never any good at it. The only other time they drank at lunch, the last time they had lunch, they ended up in bed for the first time in ten years. Today, when Sam suggests that they have rum and tonics, since he's just gotten back from the Bahamas where he drank them every day for three months, she knows he's really trying to say: The reason I haven't called you before this is that I've been away, far away, in the Bahamas. She knows he's also saying: I have no intention of going back to work today; how about you? And she knows he's probably thinking: It doesn't matter much what happens today because I'll be gone in a few weeks. But she orders a rum and tonic anyway. She is the one who should drink hemlock, she thinks; she might as well.

"What have you been up to, Cat?" He spears his wedge of lime with a green plastic stick shaped like a trident and holds it poised over his glass. "Doing any writing lately?"

This is something she began when they lived together. She's had a few things published. She looks at him for a second and then beyond him to the steeply angled glass wall of the bank building on the opposite corner, where the yellow-and-white table umbrellas they sit beneath are reproduced and strangely multiplied. She adjusts the tone of her voice to that of someone reciting from memory.

"Three years before abortion became legal, Laura became pregnant. The day this was confirmed was just four weeks after Tom had said: 'We're getting somewhere, Laura Brackman.

We're getting there.' And two weeks after all was over between them. She could never remember exactly what was said on this second occasion, except that, after a silence, he had begun with, 'I don't know what to say, but . . .' "

Sam is not amused. Nor should he be. Maybe they shouldn't be having lunch. Maybe she does need more time. He eats the lime, looks away, then looks back at Catherine. "This is what you've been writing?" She says nothing. Stern, and concerned, he asks, "Fact?"

"Fiction," she says. "No one was actually pregnant."

He leaves an angry silence, then says, "Why Tom? Why not come right out and say Sam? Or let me pick a name for myself. How about Martin? I've always been partial to Martin." But after another minute, he touches her hand again. "Besides, it wasn't all over between them. And it's not."

After a silence of her own, Catherine says—she can't help herself—"Could you be a little more specific? Could you please tell me exactly what that means?"

The muscles around his mouth tighten. She can hear silence gathering within him, as if he were piling up stones inside. Chink, chink, chink. The waiter appears from behind just then and sweeps their glasses away. Without consulting Catherine, Sam orders for both of them: the steamed mussels with parsley and thyme, and a bottle of white wine.

"You hate mussels," she says, when the waiter leaves them.

"*You* hate mussels."

"Am I being punished?" She is pleased that he remembers she hates mussels. "I think this will hurt you a lot more than it will me." After a minute, they both start laughing and the two women at the next table swing around and stare. The last thing they expected from *that* table was laughter.

When they fall silent again, Catherine wonders if she should mention the piece of pulp clinging to Sam's mustache, then decides not to, as she thinks it might give her a slight edge.

But she contemplates the piece of pulp without emotion. Maybe you have to be married to someone for a piece of pulp clinging to his mustache to irritate you, to disgust. Sam's thick dark hedge of a mustache is another thing she always loved about him. It has never varied in size or shape in all the years she has known him, although one or two tender shoots of gray have sprung up here and there. She wonders if it would be easier for her if he had shaved it off. And, suddenly, for the first time, she understands why Delilah took a razor to Samson's hair. Why should he have all that power? Why should he?

IN APRIL SHE DIDN'T have to wait very long before she knew he was not coming and, worse, that he had never intended to come. And she knew why, too. It had been her suggestion that they meet, which was a violation of usual procedure, and she had suggested it at the end of their previous meeting, another serious deviation, as it lent a taint of premeditation to these casual, occasional lunches. They never saw each other two weeks in a row, or two months in a row, or every three months or even every four. That would make Sam uncomfortable on the rare occasions when he ran into Catherine and her husband at other people's houses, or when he came to their house with other people. That had always been Sam's definition of sin: to be made uncomfortable.

She was aware of all of this in March when, getting out of his car at her bus stop, she mentioned that she had the following Wednesday afternoon off. He didn't answer right away, but she did not withdraw her suggestion. Instead, she rephrased it. "All right," he said, finally, then squeezed her elbow briefly, got back into his car, and drove away. There was an unusually decisive tone to his "all right," which entirely changed the meaning of the words, but which she did not hear until the following Wednesday when she sat waiting for him. She understood then that he had never intended to come. He had not argued with her, because that was not his way. His way was to let her sit and wait, thinking about why he wasn't there.

"Where were you?" she says suddenly. "Why weren't you there?"

"Come on, Cat." He looks her full in the eyes. "Don't."

The real reason, she knows, is that he finally said it, what he had never said to her when they lived together. Last March, before she got out of his car, before she mentioned seeing him again the next week, he finally said, "I love you." When Catherine, thinking she must have imagined the words or wished them into existence, said nothing, he let go of the steering wheel and reached for her hand. "You do know that, don't you? I don't say it, not in words. But other things should tell you. Other things should tell you that."

"Do you know what this is?" she says now, careful to keep her voice just as quiet as his. "This is a Beckett play. Every embrace is followed by a shove."

"Look." He takes a deep breath. "If I didn't really want to be here right now I would not be here, believe me. And I assume the same is true for you? Yes?" When she looks away, he takes hold of her wrist as if he would strangle it. "Why can't that be enough for you? Why?"

Catherine's husband's secretary is looking at them from the corner where she waits for the light to change. She looks the other way quickly and crosses the street, dangerously enough, against the light. Sam releases Catherine's wrist. "Who was that?"

"It's never been enough," she says. "Never."

AT LUNCH IN MARCH he asked about her family and she took from an envelope some photographs she had selected the night before: three or four showing her children to advantage, and one family snapshot taken by her sister, in which Catherine appeared to advantage but seemed remote, removed, not very happy. Sam lingered over that one and then came back to it after handing over the others. He tapped it with a finger. "Who was the dummy, anyway?" he asked.

"This is a point on which we differ," she said, reaching for the photograph, which he deftly pocketed, as she had hoped he would, buttoning it into the left breast pocket of one of those shirts. She knew he didn't mean that she was a dummy for marrying her husband instead of him, because that was not a choice that had been offered to her. He meant she was a dummy for thinking she had to be married at all, for not knowing, as he did, that marriage was bound to lead to misery.

When she wrote to tell him she was getting married—she was writing to all her old friends, she told herself, why not him?—he wrote right back. He'd been gone for several years then. He said in his letter that he had always known marriage was somehow necessary for her in a way he could never understand, and he hoped she would be very happy. Two weeks later he sent her five tall wine goblets—"Five!" her sister had said. "What kind of person would send somebody five wine glasses?"—wrapped in wads of tissue and packed inside a big black lacquered antique hatbox from an old Chicago milliner. There was a card tucked inside: "I apologize if this is too fancy, or immodest. S." At the wedding he told her that he had found the hatbox first, but then had second thoughts about sending her an empty box, although the goblets were not really his style.

Eleven years later, Catherine still has the card and the hatbox. The goblets her husband broke one night after Sam had come over to watch the Democratic National Convention on television with them. Catherine was careful not to protest as the goblets—which were not the real present, anyway—were dropped one by one from the balcony of their seventh-floor apartment into the parking lot from which Sam's vintage green MG had just exited. She said not a word, and toward morning, her husband woke her up to apologize.

SHE CRIED AT HER wedding, just seeing Sam again. Whatever had made her think she could invite him to her wedding? Whatever had made her think she could marry one man when there was another standing not five feet away—it was a small, informal wedding at home, such as people were having then—who made her weep, just to look at him, just to hear him speak? But she went through with it, as people who are not characters in movies always do, even though she was already asking herself, My God what am I doing? when she was supposed to be saying, I do, and had to be asked again. That night, her wedding night, she dreamed she was circling round and round the walls of a fortress, or maybe a cathedral. The stone was warm to the touch and she could hear voices inside. She circled round and round, feeling the walls for a hidden seam. But there was no way in.

It was another six months before she began to cry, erratically and without warning, the tears taking her by surprise in the most improbable places, at the most inconvenient times, so that she never went out, not even to the movies, without dark glasses. Sam had moved back to D.C. at the time of her wedding, which is how he had happened to be there. But she put off calling him until a year had passed. For whole months, her major activity of each day, despite a fairly responsible job with the EPA, was not calling information for Sam's telephone number. Then, one morning, some large print in the *Washington Post* caught her eye: ARE YOU STILL GRIEVING OVER A LOSS SUFFERED MORE THAN A YEAR AGO? This was apparently a sign of severe emotional disturbance. There were nine other signs listed; anyone evidencing one or more of these signs was urged to dial the telephone number at the bottom of the ad. But Catherine had called information instead, and dialed Sam's number.

It was fairly early in the morning and she woke him up. She could tell by his voice. He asked her if anything was wrong. She said no, nothing, she was fine, she just wanted to talk to him, she wanted to see him. He said he would call her later from his office when he had his calendar in front of him. She understood by that that he was not alone, and she said that would be fine. But she had barely hung up when he called back.

"Are you really fine? Are you really all right? Do you just want to see me sometime, or do you want to see me right now? Because if you do, I will come right now."

"Then come."

But when he came, all the way across town at morning rush hour, she felt awkward and inconvenient. She told him she didn't have a good reason, not even a reasonably good excuse. "You don't need one," he said. "Are we buddies or not? Are we friends?" He put his arms around her and held her, rocking her from side to side and patting her back. Then he held her away from him and looked her up and down. "Just as I suspected. You haven't been eating your carrots." He led her to the kitchen and surveyed the contents of her refrigerator, then started handing things out to her: eggs, cheese, butter, an onion, jam, bacon, some bagels.

"My therapy," he said, "always begins with a good breakfast. I'll cook. You put on some traveling music. And *not* Roberta Flack."

Roberta Flack always made them sad. They used to go to hear her sing at Mr. Henry's, the bar where she got her start, the bar right around the corner from Sam's flat, and sometimes between sets Roberta Flack would sit with them—she took turns sitting with all the regulars—and let them buy her a drink. Catherine never listened to her anymore; she didn't dare.

They carried their plates out to the balcony her husband

would one day drop the wine goblets from, and sat in the sun. They talked for several hours, about their jobs and about politics and about what they'd been reading and about various of their friends, before Sam said he really did have to get to work. He never once asked her what was wrong, as if it were entirely natural that she should be unhappy. She had gone and gotten married, hadn't she? What did she expect?

But she was no longer unhappy, she realized after he had let himself out. She had not lost him. He was still in her life, and always would be now, because now they were buddies, now they were friends. When they had been lovers his old friends had always come first. She had liked them, his old friends, but envied them their place in his heart. If one turned up in the middle of the night needing a bed, she had been put out, driven to the house in Georgetown she nominally shared with four other women. If one called from Chicago, needing help, he left her alone in his bed to set off on a thousand-mile drive through the night. But now she had joined their ranks. Now he had left someone else in his bed to rush to her aid. She had entirely by accident stumbled upon a secret entrance. She was inside. He would never make her unhappy again. He would be the one to comfort her. Wasn't it better that way? Wasn't it? Wasn't it enough?

For a while it was. But five years later she was looking for her own analyst, who had not really helped at all. She was intelligent enough in other ways but seemed never to have even heard of love. She once told Catherine that she was like the curator of an empty museum. Worse, that she was locked inside and liking it. "Who is Sam, after all?" she asked, "but the one who didn't come through?"

SAM IS TALKING ABOUT the Bahamas, describing the brilliant sky and sea, the lush vegetation, the dangers of tromping through mangrove swamps. He describes the remote outer islands and the government's recent efforts to improve transportation among them. Catherine understands that he was working there in some capacity, but doesn't want to ask any questions that will betray the fact that she has not really been listening.

The waiter brings their steamed mussels, handling the plates with thick, folded napkins, and warns them to be careful. He opens the wine and pours a little into Sam's glass, and waits. Sam finishes what he is saying, which takes a minute or two, then waves a hand, impatient at being interrupted. "Just pour it," he says. The waiter pours Catherine's wine and fills Sam's glass, then plunges the bottle deep into the wine cooler and stalks off.

"Why did you do that?" Catherine says, then quotes something her father once said to her when she behaved badly. "Rudeness to people who serve you is the mark of a peasant."

"Who told you that?" Sam says. "It's not true."

"When are you leaving?"

He looks at her quickly, but she looks again at the glass wall of the bank building on the opposite corner, where the reflection of the yellow-and-white table umbrellas they sit beneath wavers all too liquidly now. Sam covers her hand with his, presses it.

"You heard."

"Yes. I heard."

"I was going to tell you, later. I didn't want to spoil our lunch. I'm leaving at the end of the month. I start the second week of August. A new job, unbelievable money."

"Great," Catherine says. "Have a lobster. Have a crab."

"I'll be based in L.A. but I'll still be in and out of town, three or four times a year. It won't make any difference, Cat. It won't change a thing."

"That's what I'm afraid of."

* * *

"IN THIRTY YEARS MORE, this will be the same," he said in March, as, arm in arm and a little drunk, they waited to leap from the curb at the corner of Connecticut and M. "Only we'll be old then and cardiac arrest will be a more immediate worry. And will we indeed be able to walk when the sign says WALK?"

A modest fantasy, but Sam does not usually deal in futures of any kind, and so this made Catherine happy. They walked a little farther together, as their paths lay in the same direction, her office, his car. On N Street Catherine pointed out the house where Franklin Roosevelt lived when he was Secretary of the Navy, the house where he met the woman, not Eleanor, he would love for the rest of his life. (See? she told herself. You're not the only one. This happens to other people. No one ever said Franklin Roosevelt was a lunatic.) She pointed out the house and told Sam the part of their story that happened there. When she finished he kissed the top of her head. But at the next corner he stopped and faced her.

"What did you mean telling me that story?"

"I didn't *mean* anything, and it's not a story. It's true. It's history. It's common knowledge."

"You made it up," he said. "Never mind. It's still a good story."

He stopped beside an unfamiliar gray car, a much-used and elderly Porsche. When he took out his keys and she realized the car belonged to him, Catherine instantly missed the old green MG, the car whose rapidly diminishing roar she still hears sometimes in her dreams. They stood beside the Porsche in silence for several minutes, unwilling to part, uncertain as to how to proceed. Then he put a hand on her shoulder and lifted his eyes to the sky for a second. "Blessed are the poor in taste. Therefore, let me say this." He stood squarely before her, his eyes on her eyes, and spoke quietly.

"It is now well after two o'clock, and as I see it we have two options open to us. We can be sensible and go back to work with conscience clear. Or, we can be foolish, which we'll most likely regret almost immediately. I, for one, would much prefer to be foolish. But I don't want to have to think about it. And I certainly don't want to talk about it."

This was another thing about him. It wasn't just the voice itself but what the voice said that Catherine loved. When she lived with him, when he was an impoverished Latin teacher, he often incorporated Latin words and phrases into his conversation, and he always had a courteous, courtly way of discerning her preferences, even if it was just between two television shows. He would turn on *Mission Impossible* and, instead of asking if it was okay with her, would say something like, "Placetne?"

Catherine did not want to be sensible either, nor did she want to have to think about it, and he made it easy for her by unlocking the passenger door and holding it open. "Placetne?" he asked. "Placetne, Magistra?"

Yes, it pleased her.

NOW SHE THINKS ABOUT the various places where he has lived. The G Street flat with its grilled windows and padlocked doors, where she was always afraid of being trapped in a fire, and where he evidently was afraid of being trapped by her. Then there was, briefly, a canal barge, then the summer guesthouse, then the attic of the old Merriweather Post mansion where his rent had been greatly reduced in exchange for keeping an eye on things and where, shades of Gatsby, they had one afternoon waltzed to silent music in the derelict ballroom. And then the long white basement room he had taken her to in March. Bare floors, a narrow bed in a raw wooden frame, even a concave niche in the wall above, where he had put his watch to keep vigil over them.

A monk's cell, Catherine thinks now. Money has made no difference in his life; there is still no room in it for anyone else.
Why did she want so badly to get in?

She remembers a story he told her years before, how he was
shocked and saddened on his return to Chicago to find that his
undergraduate advisor, a man he would have entrusted with his
life, had killed himself, had put over his head one black plastic
trash bag after another, until there were too many to claw his
way through in time, then fastened them with a rope. The note
he left behind said only, "Satis est satis." That's exactly what
Catherine is thinking now: enough is enough.

Sam unbuttons the left breast pocket of his immaculate
khaki shirt and withdraws one of the new business cards he
picked up at the printers near Catherine's office, and hands it to
her. She is careful not to read what it says.

"We're moving too," she says, laying the card on the table.

"Where to this time? Another invitation from afar?" Twice
since her marriage, her husband has spent a year at British uni-
versities and she, of course, went with him.

"Iowa. We're leaving for good this time. We're putting the
house on the market." When Sam says nothing, seeming incapable of speech, she goes on. "It's a good offer. It's something he's
always wanted."

Sam still says nothing.

"He left it up to me to decide, since I'll have to quit my job.
It was my decision. Washington is not a good place for kids."

"Jesus! You want to do that? You want to give up your job?
You must be crazy, Cat. What would you do out there?"

"I thought I'd go back to school, get an M.A., maybe even
a doctorate. Then I could teach."

Sam takes out the one cigarette a day he still allows himself
and lights it, releasing the smoke in two angry jets across the
table. "I would never leave it up to you to decide, if this is the

kind of decision you come up with. Never." They sit in silence for a while. When he finishes his cigarette he stubs it out with one sharp twist of his thumb. "I'm not going there, you know," he says. "I am never going to Iowa."

"I know that."

But she doesn't really believe that this will be the last time she will see him and the only time she will see him with any clarity. She doesn't know that in the university town where she will live for the next dozen years, where she now believes there will be nothing to remind her of this man, the local supermarket chain, its name emblazoned in huge red letters all over town, will be SAM'S. And she doesn't know that in the place where her faculty friends will gather on Friday afternoons there will be an old jukebox full of old records, including Roberta Flack's "That's No Way to Say Good-bye," or that often on Friday afternoons a lonely man in the political science department will drink too much and play that song over and over and that she will sit and listen to it and remember—in spite of all the new things she'll be learning—how one night at Mr. Henry's she and Sam confessed that "That's No Way to Say Good-bye" was their favorite song, and how, before she sang it toward the end of her last set, Roberta Flack had smiled and pointed a jeweled forefinger at them and said into the mike in her black velvet voice, "This song is *yours*."

And because she doesn't know any of these things, because she can't guess, when Sam goes inside to find the men's room, Catherine gets up and leaves.

Everything Goes

Frank watches from the doorway as Linda cleans out her mother's dresser drawers, most of which have not been opened in the past year. She moves through them with the same efficiency with which she has gone through the rest of the house, making swift decisions before consigning each object to one of three piles on the bed behind her: things she wants to keep for herself; things she will send to one of her three brothers or their wives, who have already left, carting with them various pieces of furniture, lamps, rugs, and a fair portion of photographs ("Okay." Linda spread a batch of photographs on the kitchen table. "These are all Mom's baby pictures. Everybody put your finger on your favorite one."); and things to be thrown away. This last pile seems to consist entirely of Emma's underthings, a cottony-silky jumble in black and white from which Frank keeps his eyes averted.

But it's not Emma he is thinking about now. He's found that he doesn't have to think about Emma. She is still with him in some essential way, a constant presence, or a merely temporary absence: she is just downstairs, or upstairs, in the next room. He has been wondering if it will be that way in California, if Emma will be there too, or if she'll stay behind. But right now it's Linda he's thinking about, Linda thirty years ago, emptying the drawers of another dresser while he watched from another doorway. That time she was moving a lot faster and making no decisions whatever, simply yanking out each drawer and dumping its entire contents into one of several waiting suitcases, Frank tapping his foot and looking at his watch every thirty seconds. They both wanted to get the hell out of there before her husband came home for lunch.

He and Emma had known Linda was unhappy, had known from the start she would have to be miserable, given the jackass she was marrying. But once married she never complained and it was the bishop, oddly enough, who finally alerted them, calling the house one morning before Frank had left for the office, before he was even out of bed. "Mr. Kimmerling," he'd said, in a sober, tired voice. "Your daughter's got herself in a terrible situation over here. You'd better come and get her." Frank had put down the phone and turned to Emma, who hovered nearby, a hand still at the throat of her nightgown, where it had flown at the words "I'll be right there," and told her he was going to get Linda and bring her home.

Driving the fifty-some miles to the town where Linda was living, it occurred to Frank he had no idea what he would find when he got there. He hadn't asked the bishop a single question, because, in a way, he'd been waiting for such a telephone call for over a year, ever since Linda's wedding day, when he and Emma had heard her sobbing behind the closed door of her bedroom. He did wonder what particular crisis might have brought the bishop to Linda's house at that hour of the morning, if the call had in fact been made from Linda's house, but he pictured no bloody scene, no cuts, bruises, swellings, no beatings during the night. If he was afraid of anything, it was that he might find his son-in-law on the floor weeping. Frank had no use for the asshole, but he *was* certain he was incapable of violence and would never deliberately hurt Linda in any way.

What then were his sins? Small things leapt to mind. He often probed an ear with a Q-tip in the presence of other people. He had bought Emma (and Linda, and Linda's grand-mother) a succession of plastic flower arrangements. At a joint family dinner he had produced a father and brother who, in 1965, wore their hair parted in the middle and plastered with some kind of dark grease. At their first meeting he had called Frank's grandfather (a man—a German immigrant—of enor-mous dignity) "grandpaw" and told him he had played his hand of cards like a sausage, as in "you played that one like a sausage, Grandpaw."

Linda had disliked these things every bit as much as Frank had. But to offset them were country club dances driven to in a white convertible with the top down on fine midwestern summer nights, dinners at expensive restaurants, a private plane that flew her to Chicago for the symphony and opera, for an evening at the Pump Room, for shopping. She was a junior in college. He—what the hell was his name, anyway? Frank's chil-dren have married so many people, how can he be expected to remember their names?—was twelve years older, with a good job and lots of money. At Christmas he gave Linda a diamond ring. Several of her sorority sisters got engaged that same Christmas, but none of them had a rock anything like the size of Linda's and she did not want to give it back.

Two months after the engagement, Frank got a phone call from his prospective son-in-law who said he had heard Linda was still dating "down there," which was how he always referred to the state university, located three hundred miles away in the southern part of the state. He wanted Linda to withdraw from school and live at home so they could see more of each other and decide whether or not they were to be married. He used those exact words, "whether or not we are to be married." His prim, pompous tone irritated Frank, who was incensed at this request coming just one day after the deadline for withdrawing from the university with even a partial tuition refund. But he did think that if Linda were to see more of this jerk she couldn't possibly marry him, so he said that if his daughter wanted to throw away her future and come home he would not stop her, if that's what he was being asked.

But it didn't seem to Frank they actually did see more of each other. Linda's fiancé lived those fifty-some miles away. He was a bank vice-president, thirty-two years old and prematurely set in his ways. He had Kiwanis on Monday nights, and something else on Tuesdays and Wednesdays and Thursdays. He made no concessions to being engaged to (in Frank's opinion) a beautiful, talented and lively girl of twenty, who could have been out every night of the week if she chose, and who could have been anything she wanted to be if she stayed in school and got her degree. Instead, Linda chose a mindless filing job in Frank's office and spent her week nights sitting at home with her parents or grandparents or great-grandparents playing cards, playing the piano, watching television. (All her girlfriends were away at school; boys were out of the question.) But on weekends there were the dances, the dinners, the trips to Chicago, the looking at houses, the shopping for furniture and china and silver. There were the engagement parties, the presents.

"What would we do with all the presents?"

When Frank heard Linda sobbing behind her bedroom door on the morning of her wedding he went in and tried to talk her out of it. So did Emma. They begged her to call it off, to let them call it off for her. Frank said he would go down to the church and tell everyone to go home. He said he wouldn't mind doing that; he said nothing would give him greater pleasure. A look of wild hope had flashed in Linda's eyes, already dazzled with tears, but was gone in an instant and she was sobbing again. "What would we do with all the presents?" Frank and Emma assured her that presents were the last thing to be considered at such a moment, that presents could be sent back at any time but a marriage was forever. They believed that, and

Linda believed that, then. But she went through with it just the same, and a year later there was Frank, going to bring her home.

He did not find his son-in-law on the floor weeping. His son-in-law wasn't even home; he didn't know Linda was going to leave him. Neither did Linda. She had been making chicken salad for her husband's lunch and was surprised when she opened the door and saw her father with a suitcase in each hand. But when he told her he was there to take her back home, that same look of wild hope lit up her eyes.

She was wearing jeans and red sneakers, her dark hair pulled high into a pert ponytail. She looked so young running, jumping, ripping clothes off their hangers and sweeping boxes off the closet shelves, scooping up armfuls of shoes. She looked like a little girl, a child who should have been in school in the middle of a Wednesday morning, not playing house in some grown man's kitchen. And a little girl who ought to be in school, Frank reflected, was exactly what she was.

She took nothing but her clothes, he noticed. She didn't even glance at anything else, not one of the hundreds of doo-dads and whatnots and knickknacks she had wasted a whole college semester acquiring, not one of the presents for which she had written more than two hundred thank-you notes. She showed not a hint of regret for anything she was leaving behind. Even her diamond ring; when she was locking the front door, Frank saw she was still wearing it and told her the ring had to stay. She whipped it off without a second's hesitation, the wedding band too; she opened the door and tossed the rings onto the elaborate marquetry surface of the satinwood console table that stood just inside the front door, and Frank had to admit that maybe she had learned something after all.

It's only now, thirty years later, that he finds himself wondering what the bishop's role in all that was. Frank and Emma knew at the time that Linda had been talking to the bishop, who had once been a priest in the Kimmerlings' parish and had known Linda since she was a child. Linda had told them how kind he had been to her, how he would always see her whenever she needed to talk to someone. But was it usual for a bishop to condone, to encourage, even to instigate a divorce on the grounds that the wife had decided she could not, after all, abide the sight of her husband cleaning out his ears with Q-tips? Maybe it was the bishop who'd gotten himself in a terrible situation over there.

Frank considers asking her about it. If he did, she would tell him. They are no longer like parent and child, but two adults. If anything, their roles have been reversed. Instead of Frank going to bring Linda home after a bad marriage, something he has had to do more than once, it's Linda, now that Frank's marriage is over, who has come to take him to live with her, in California, which seems to Frank a lot farther away from home than the place where Emma has gone.

But he decides not to ask her about the bishop. She might get the wrong idea, might think he's been harboring some suspicion all these years, or brooding about some unsavory aspect of her character. She might think he means to judge her in some way when he is merely curious, merely wanting to fit the missing piece into an old puzzle. But he would lose far more than he would gain by asking that question. He asks another one instead. He addresses the back of Linda's head.

"What was his name? That jerk you were married to?"

Her hair is cut too short for a ponytail, but she still wears jeans and sneakers, although Frank has seen her, on visits to Los Angeles, emerge from her back-bedroom office in a dark suit and high heels, carrying a briefcase, rushing off to the airport to conduct one of her meetings, "seminars" she calls them. She's standing at the dresser rooting through a round box of faded pink Frank remembers giving to Emma when the satin covering was thick and plush and its color a deep rose. Absorbed in the contents of the box, Linda responds absently.

"Which jerk?"

"The first one."

She doesn't turn around but looks up and catches Frank's eye in the mirror hanging at a slant over the dresser. Her own hazel eyes are still bright. Frank has noticed something called Eyebright among the arsenal of vitamins and herbs she swallows every morning; this may have something to do with the undiminished spark in her eyes. But now a cloud passes over them.

"Oh, Dad! How could you forget that name? And you saw him at the funeral. Don't you remember?" There is that speculative tone, that diagnostic look that people her age take on whenever they ask people his age if they don't remember something.

"Of course I remember the funeral," he snaps. "I just forgot the asshole's goddamn name for Christ's sake!" Careful now, he tells himself. Careful. And to show that he doesn't really lose his temper that easily, that he's not going to embarrass her every time she turns around, he grins at his daughter's reflection in the mirror. Uncertain, she smiles briefly, then bends her head to the box again.

FRANK STARTS DOWN THE stairs to scare up some lunch for them, leftovers from the fancy meals one of his daughters-in-law has cooked over the past week. They are a strange lot, his daughters-in-law. One of them never cooks a goddamn thing and one of them never stops cooking. Cooking or shopping or copying recipes or looking them up on her computer to see how much damage they'll do. One of them never eats. Have people always been this way, overboard in everything? Food used to be such a simple thing. Mostly you were just glad to get some when you were hungry.

"Dad, wait. What's this?" Linda comes out of the bedroom holding up a little button, like a campaign button. "I HAVE SEEN THE FUTURE. What's that supposed to mean?"

"Your mother." He takes the button from her and holds it in the palm of his hand; he stares at it as if it is a crystal ball containing not the future—who wants to see that anymore?—but the past. Emma, prettier at eighteen than even Linda could ever have dreamed of being, in her light blue dress and open-toed shoes, a little white hat, gloves, her eyes wide and lips parted, looking up at the giant silver letters, G M, with the narrow opening between them, the door into the future.

"The Futurama," he explains. "It was a ride at the World's Fair. We went on our honeymoon. It was an exhibit, not a ride, but you rode through it. It was your mother's favorite thing." They were so eager to be inside that building, to see what was in store, and see it again, they were willing to wait all day and willing to do it all over again the next day, and the next. The fourth day, Emma went in alone; Frank couldn't take standing in line for six or seven hours one more time. God, how his feet ached. No such thing then as cushioned walking shoes, which Frank thinks of not as shoes at all, but as a form of transportation.

"The New York World's Fair," he says, and after a minute adds, "1939."

Frank hears the clarinet player who was stationed at the bottom of the two winding ramps to entertain the silent hordes inching their way like an army of ants across the concrete face of the General Motors building. "Anything Goes." He must have heard a few other songs in six or seven hours; there must have been a change of musicians over three or four days. But Frank hears that one clarinet playing that one song, "Anything Goes." He smells the air, the heavy, humid eastern air, the exotic smell of the salt sea. Frank, who had no idea then he'd

soon be freighted across the Atlantic in a troop ship under conditions not much better than the ones his grandfather had
endured, had never smelled the sea before.

"Come on." Linda takes hold of his arm, startling him. "I'll
get you some lunch."

AT THE FUNERAL HOME Frank was startled to find his elbow
grabbed and then his hand being wrung by a man he'd never
seen before. In his sixties, maybe, the man wore an expensive
gray silk suit, just like the undertaker's, and, also like the undertaker, he pressed one of Frank's hands between both of his. His
gray hair, combed straight back from his forehead, had dark
ridges made by a wet or greasy comb. He stunk of musk, a smell
Frank finds nauseating, and told Frank he was sorry for his
trouble, that Emma had been a wonderful woman, wonderful,
wonderful. He reminded Frank of Lawrence Welk.

"Thank you," Frank said. "Thank you for coming," which
was what he said to nearly everyone.

"You don't remember me, do you?" There was no accusation, no surprise, just a statement. "I'm Frank. Frank Jordan."

"Of course," Frank said, extracting his hand from the other
man's damp grasp. "Good of you to come." But the name meant
nothing to him.

Later that night, when the kids were sitting around the
kitchen table with plates of food and a bottle of rye, he heard
the boys teasing Linda and realized the man who had shaken his
hand in that fulsome way had once been his son-in-law. To
think they might still be related, to think Frank might have
Lawrence Welk for a son-in-law! Lawrence Welk or the one she
married next, that good-looking good-for-nothing who led her
to hell and back before going to prison for drugs.

Frank wandered into the TV room just off the kitchen, eased

himself back in one of the two matching recliners, closed his eyes and pretended to sleep. He had always enjoyed listening to his children talk and reminisce and knew they wouldn't talk as freely if he was in the same room with them; they might think he would disapprove of their stories or laughter, or believe them to be lacking in respect for their mother, although no one liked to hear them talk and laugh more than she did.

This time Frank heard a story he'd never heard before, one Linda and Bobby, his youngest son, were telling for the benefit of their newest sister-in-law. It was about the time Bobby went over to stay with Linda for a week during the summer after her first wedding. Bobby was still in high school and doing mostly odd jobs that summer and Linda's husband had hired him, as a favor to Linda, to do some painting. Frank had always known all that, but he had never heard how the painting job had come to an abrupt end, or even that it *had* come to an abrupt end. He'd always thought Bobby had simply finished the job and come home.

"I was painting the dining room," Bobby said, "and making a pretty good job of it, if I do say so. I'd finished three walls and the ceiling, the baseboards, the trim. It was late and it was hot, so I opened a cold one."

"He drank a whole six-pack," Linda cut in. "In half an hour."

"You had a few yourself," Bobby pointed out.

"He painted a huge head on the fourth wall, a man's head with a Q-tip sticking out of each ear."

"Then we heard the garage door going up."

"I panicked," Linda said. "I was frantic."

"What are you talking about? You were laughing. You couldn't stop laughing."

"He wouldn't do anything," Linda said. "He just stood there drinking his beer, a big smirk on his face. I took the paint brush and started splashing paint on the wall, trying to cover it up.

The paint got all over the place. On me, the baseboards, the floor. It was green paint and the baseboards were white."

"You were pretty drunk."

"I was not! I was frantic."

"So what does the asshole do when he comes in?" Bobby said, laughing. "He doesn't even say hello. He goes straight into the downstairs bathroom and we can hear him brushing his teeth and gargling."

"Why?" This was one of the sisters-in-law, the one who neither eats nor drinks and seems to disapprove of both activities. "Had he been drinking too?"

"No!" Linda almost shrieked. "That's what he did every day. He came home and went straight into the bathroom to brush his teeth, gargle and clean out his ears."

"He did," Bobby chimed in. "I was there for five days. He did the same thing every day."

"So while I was getting supper—it was all ready," Linda said, "I just had to put it on the table—Bobby goes into the bathroom to clean up and he comes out with his hair parted in the middle and all slicked down, and he has a Q-tip sticking straight out of each ear."

"So you got fired?" The voice belonged to the newest sister-in-law.

"Not then," Bobby said. "Not until he saw the mess *she* made in the dining room."

"EARTH TO DAD," LINDA says in the cheerful voice of a nurse. She's standing at the refrigerator with the door open. "Did you hear me? Do you want the pasta or the couscous?"

"Couscous," he says, to show he can keep up with the times, although he really wants the pasta. The jerk's name was Frank. Frank! No wonder she thought he was senile for forgetting it.

All his children already think he's senile for taking thirty thousand less for this house than he was offered. But he liked the young couple who made the first offer, liked to think of them living in this house, putting their children to bed in the same rooms where Frank and his brothers and then Frank's children have slept. He could tell they really loved the house and would live as much of their lives in it as the times would permit. The guy who offered him thirty thousand more was older, in his forties, and knew a good thing when he saw it. He'd make a few improvements then turn around and sell for a tidy profit. And he was condescending and sycophantic, treating Frank like a child, fawning over him and touching his arm.

The man had been extolling the pristine condition of the house, built by Frank's father in 1901, and saying with phony reverence how this or that had been here for more than ninety years or been used for almost a century. And it is true that much of the original leaded glass remains in the windows and that the woodwork and doors throughout the house are of the original varnished oak; the brass switch plates on the ground floor have the original mother-of-pearl buttons you push to turn the ceiling fixtures on and off. But the columned front porch was added twenty years later, Frank told the man, and the pine floors were replaced by hardwood sometime during the twenties. A coal furnace was installed in 1914. In 1945 the entire heating system was replaced, although coal was still used. A dry sink and all of the original kitchen cupboards were torn out in 1947 and a new double sink put in. In 1960 a second bathroom was added. A bay window was installed in the kitchen alcove, making what is now the breakfast room. The sliding doors between the living room and dining room were removed. The coal furnace was converted to gas.

And changes outside the house kept pace. The back yard used to end in cornfields, stretching to open country. Now there are other houses, other streets, miles and miles of them, all opened up after the war. The brick street in front of the house was paved over in 1937 and then again after the streetcar tracks were pulled up in 1940, as public transportation moved from horse cars to streetcars to buses.

"Imagine him knowing all that!" The man spoke not to Frank but to Frank's son Peter. "Imagine him remembering all those facts." He leaned over Frank's chair as if he was thinking of patting Frank on the head. "I'll bet you miss those streetcars."

"The hell I do," Frank said. "They were goddamn noisy. Clanging and rattling and screeching." Then he got up and walked out of the room.

"FRANK," HE SAYS OUT loud. "Frank Jordan. That was his name."

But Linda doesn't hear. Attracted by two bright cardinals at the feeder hanging outside the kitchen window over the sinks, she stands looking out. Then the beeper on the microwave sounds and she takes Frank's plate and sets it in front of him. "Will you be all right here for a few minutes? A half hour? I need some exercise."

"Eat your lunch," Frank barks, without meaning to, then adjusts his tone. "You've been exercising all morning. You should sit down."

"Cleaning out drawers is not exercise. I need a walk, and I'm not hungry."

"Go on then, go on." Is he barking again? Are those tears in her eyes? He waves her away in the direction of the back door, then lifts his hand, smiles. She smiles back. At fifty she is a damn handsome woman, with a slim figure and a deep glossy shine to her dark hair, and Frank is grateful to her for making the effort he knows these things must cost. His sons have either put on too much weight or lost too much, lost muscle tone, lost

their hair, or turned gray. Nothing he and Emma saw in that
Futurama prepared them for having old men for their children.

"You'll be all right?" Linda pauses with her hand on the
knob. "Are you sure?"

"Of course I'm sure."

But how can he be sure? How can anyone? Nobody was
expected back in a few minutes or a half hour when he had
what his doctor refers to now as his "episode," as if Frank's heart
attack was some kind of staged melodrama. Yet he survived. He
dialed the correct number, gave the correct information,
unlocked the front door, and lay down in the hall to wait. While
Emma, with no warning, not even a sound, was snatched away
with Frank sitting right next to her.

"Frank, you look dead tired," Emma said. "Why don't you
pull over and let me drive for a while?" It was a Sunday night
and they were on their way back from a weekend visit to Roy's.
Roy had given his share of trouble—they all had—but he ended
up okay. "You kids really know how to lay it on, don't you?"
Emma had said to him the night he called to tell them he had
left his first wife, a girl he'd known all his life and whose parents
were Frank and Emma's oldest friends, although both of them
are dead now. "Wait just a minute," Roy had said. "If you think
I'm doing this to punish you, you are sadly mistaken. This has
nothing to do with you. Nothing." Frank could have strangled
him.

But all that was years behind them. Peace had long been
made and they'd just had a good weekend visit with Roy and his
"new" wife of fifteen years, the one who cooks all the time. It
was just the four of them—Roy's children are all grown, in college—and they played a lot of cards, just as Frank and Emma
used to do with Frank's parents.

"I really enjoyed that," Emma said, as they drove away from
Roy's house. "That was a good visit."

Frank had been driving for three hours when Emma said he looked tired and offered to drive for a while, so he pulled over the first chance he got, when the highway had straightened and flattened and conditions were optimum for Emma, a cautious driver, to ease back into traffic. He stopped the car and put it in neutral. "Do you want to just slide over?" he asked her. "Or do you want to get out and stretch your legs?" But she didn't answer him, didn't even look at him. She just lurched forward suddenly, as far as her seatbelt allowed, as if there was something she was trying to see.

WHEN THEY FINALLY SNAKED their way to the top of the ramp, finally filed through that narrow opening into the future, they found themselves in a dark room and on another ramp, this one zigzagging downwards, a giant map of the United States on the far wall. Then the floor was moving beneath them. Exhausted, they fell into the high-backed, deeply cushioned chairs that came along to transport them into the distant year of 1960. Frank remembers the deep, dramatic voice piped into the back of each chair, remembers the thrill that first time he heard the command, "All eyes to the future!" He remembers Emma, her feet together and gloved hands folded on her knees as they embarked on their coast-to-coast flight over a scaled-down model of the United States, eagerly leaning forward to look.

What did they see?

Fruit trees growing under glass domes on a hillside, spiraling cities with glass skyscrapers and elevated sidewalks. A fabulous suspension bridge. Parks. Suburbs, a startlingly new concept in 1939 when everyone lived either on a farm or in a town. But mostly there were highways, also a new idea then. A web of superhighways traversing the country, seven lanes in each direction, cars zipping along them at improbable speeds.

Except for the suburbs and something of the cities, 1960 didn't turn out to be like that. In 1960 it still took six hours to get up to the lake in Wisconsin, driving that two-lane, backed up behind campers and trailers and overheated cars, averaging thirty, forty miles an hour. In 1960 they still drove out to Minkler's orchard on fall Sunday afternoons to pick apples and buy jugs of cider, doughnuts for the kids, who liked to kick through the leaves looking for fallen apples to throw at each other. The idea of growing apple trees under glass domes never really caught on.

They've got their superhighways now, though, Frank thinks, and cars zipping in every direction. He imagines Emma leaning forward, looking down on a model of the highway where one day her life will end, on the highway he'll be traveling with Linda the day after tomorrow, the straight, flat, empty highway with its ominous signs warning you that the next rest stop is ninety-three miles away. Frank hopes he doesn't go the way Emma did. It won't make a bit of difference to him how he goes, but he hopes he doesn't do that to Linda. He sees her, a little girl in a ponytail, frantic, driving down the highway.

"OH, DADDY," LINDA'S VOICE sags under a weight of disappointment. "You didn't eat a thing. You didn't take a single bite. What am I going to do with you?"

She picks up the plate and takes it back to the microwave. When it is heated again she sets it down in front of him and tries to pry the button from his clenched fist, the button they gave him—or Emma—when the line of moving chairs curved away from the future and they stepped off the conveyor belt and walked out into the summer day with their whole lives ahead of them.

"I have to make some phone calls." When Frank wins the tug-of-war and hangs on to the button, Linda puts her hands on her hips in exactly the same way her mother used to. "They're going to disconnect tomorrow and I have some things to take care of. When I come back I want to see this food gone, okay?"

He can't remember what it is that she does. She's explained it more than once and he doesn't like to ask her again. He'll be able to figure it out. She works mostly at home in one of the small back bedrooms of her condominium with a couple of computers, a fax machine, two telephones. That's how she's able to take him to live with her. Frank's sons and their wives all go out to work every day. He heard them discussing it when he was in the hospital. He heard every word. Nothing wrong with his ears.

"I don't know," he heard Linda say. "To move from that huge house into that tiny bedroom. It might kill him."

"It might kill you, you mean." That was Bobby.

"He could come to us for vacations," Peter's wife said. "We'd all help."

"He may be too old to live with any of us," Bobby's wife said. "He may need more care than any of us can give him." She's the one who never cooks.

"For God's sake," Linda said. "He's been living by himself for the past year."

"And look what happened."

"I want to go with you," he whispered, the first time Linda was alone with him. "I don't need much room."

And this is true. Within Frank are a multitude of rooms in which he likes to wander, mulling over this and that, finishing old uncompleted puzzles he finds lying around. Yet he knows that when it comes time to leave, when he has to lock the door of this house for the last time, he'll want to hang back, resist, refuse; he'll want to howl. But he'll go quietly, if he knows what's good for him. He's a man who has seen the future.

Dardis and Me

My sister Dardis came to live with me in London after our parents died. I'd told Dardis to stay where she was. It was the beginning of her senior year at Cornell and I told her to get her degree first, then she could do whatever she wanted. But Dardis always did whatever she wanted, and after going back to school for a few weeks she called me at four o'clock in the morning and said her nerves were shot, she couldn't concentrate, couldn't sleep, was seeing things. "When I drive at night I see people running across the road. I slam on the brakes and nobody's there. I open the car door and see snakes in the gutter."

"Maybe you shouldn't drive for a while. Take a taxi or a bus. Get someone else to drive you."

"We're orphans now, Dennis. We have to stick together."

"You are twenty-one years old and I am twenty-five. We hardly qualify as orphans." But the truth is I was feeling a little vulnerable myself. Since our parents died, an invisible shield had been smashed, a protective ozone layer disintegrated.

"Don't be ponderous, Dennis. I need you."

A month later Dardis moved into the one-bedroom flat I had been occupying alone since I started graduate work at the London School of Economics two years before. I had sublet it furnished from a pair of schoolteachers who had lived in it themselves for some years before going off to seek higher wages in New Zealand, and it was luxurious by student standards. There were curtains on the windows, carpets on the floors, pictures on the walls, books on the shelves, a heated towel rack in the bathroom.

I could see that the ordered domesticity of my life took Dardis by surprise. As I watched her run a thoughtful finger along an alphabetized shelf of books, I remembered the clutter that had always surrounded her, the trail of wet towels, the damp rings drying to white on mahogany tabletops, and I congratulated myself for my foresight in having given up the bedroom to her. I wanted Dardis where I could shut the door on her. But she wouldn't hear of it. She bounced on my bed, which I'd moved out into the sitting room and camouflaged with a black and yellow Indian throw, testing it.

"I will *not* let you give up your bed, Dennis. I'll be fine out here, really. I insist."

Resigned to the lumpy couch I'd moved into the bedroom for her, I put down her bags, deriving considerable comfort from the size of them: just one medium suitcase, a small overnight bag. That should do Dardis for about three weeks at the most. She got off the bed and started opening doors, checking the closet space.

"I shipped my trunks almost three weeks ago. They should be here any day now." Her voice was casual, but I detected a slight tremor.

"Dardis, just how long are you planning to stay?"

She put her arms around my neck and kissed me rapidly on both cheeks. The little pats that accompanied her kisses. My mother's eyes and mouth. My father's nose, his slenderness acquired suddenly by Dardis through his death as if bequeathed, a parting gift. I kissed her back.

* * *

I TOOK DARDIS OUT that night, which was a mistake, but she said she was too excited and too tired to sleep. We spent a couple of hours at a pub, during which she put away several whiskeys and water and told me about her visit to the stock-broker to discuss her half of our parents' portfolio, a word Dardis handled like a new piece of slang.

"He was such a prig, Dennis, you can't imagine. When I walked into his office he kept looking over my shoulder for someone else, as if some grown-up were parking the car and would be there any minute. He couldn't believe he had to talk to me. So I got fed up right away and told him I wanted to liq-uidate."

At dinner I ordered for both of us without asking for the wine list, but Dardis was flying and not about to deplane. "Isn't anyone going to get anything to drink?"

She jabbed at her food with a fork but ate nothing and talked nonstop, repeating herself alcoholically and growing more maudlin by the minute. Dardis never knew when to stop. Even when she was learning how to walk, she'd take off and run until she fell on her face, and everybody would laugh and say that Dardis had no brakes.

She drank the second bottle by herself and told me again how my father had died. When I was home for the funeral I had heard the story three times from Dardis, who was the only wit-ness, and each version was slightly different. All I knew for sure was that about six weeks after my mother's long-expected death from cancer, my father suffered a massive coronary in his kitchen after breakfast. The variables were what Dardis had been reading while my father cleared their plates from the table, whether or not he had managed to deposit them carefully on the counter before crashing to the floor, and whether or not he had died to spite Dardis for not offering to stay home and take care of him. Tonight, she had been reading *Death in Venice*, the plates crashed to the floor as well, and my father died because he simply could not live without my mother. I don't suppose it ever occurred to Dardis that this constant readjustment of the scene might be a little hard on me.

Outside the restaurant I looked for a taxi, but Dardis insisted on walking to a pub for a nightcap and more cigarettes. She'd already smoked a whole pack. On the way home she lay with her head in my lap, moaning from time to time, but she sat up when I paid the driver. She was sure I hadn't given him enough. She reached into her bag and thrust a fistful of dollar bills at him. When she turned away he handed them to me with a sympathetic snort. "Got a handful there, mate."

I hauled Dardis up the two flights of dark steps and switched on the light. "We're home," I said. She turned on me and shouted, "Define home," then plunged straight ahead into a coffee table, cutting her shin on a sharp glass corner. I lowered her into a chair and went to the kitchen for a pan of soap and water to wash her cut, which was a serious one, but when I came back with it she threw a lighted cigarette into the water and headed for the bathroom. I pulled out the pillows from under her bed, turned back the covers and went into my room, stretched out, and lay there listening to my sister cry herself to sleep.

WHEN I CAME HOME late the next afternoon, I had plans for Dardis. I told her I would take her skiing in Austria over Christmas on the condition that she learn German in the meantime. The German was Helen's idea, the trip to Austria was mine. Dardis loved to ski and I knew Christmas would be hard for her; I wasn't exactly looking forward to it myself. Helen got very quiet at the mention of Austria. She was a part-time instructor at LSE I'd been seeing on and off for nearly a year, and I talked to her about Dardis at lunch. "I just meant *some* sort of project," she said, "something to occupy her time, her mind. It needn't be German at all."

But Dardis was enthusiastic. She was still in her nightgown and looked as if she'd been run over by a truck. It wasn't just the hangover; contrition took her that way. When I outlined my plan she brightened perceptibly, tucked her bare feet up and sat on them. "Where do I sign?" Then her face wrinkled in apology. "I'm really sorry about last night, Dennis. I almost never do that. Never."

The next morning we went to the Goethe Institute where Dardis signed up for an eight-week intensive course in intro-ductory German scheduled to begin the following Monday. Most of the intervening days I took her with me nearly every-where so she could learn her way around. She was never without her *A to Z* and her map of the underground, which she pored over constantly, matching our routes with the colored lines in her lap. On Saturday we were supposed to meet Helen at the Tate at two o'clock. We were three tube stops away and already late when Dardis, who had been pondering the over-head map across the aisle, jumped to her feet in a panic.

"Dennis, we have to get off. We're going the wrong way. Hurry!" And I, although I knew exactly where we were, fol-lowed her off the train just as the doors slammed shut. That's what irritated me about Dardis, I realized as we waited in silence for the next train. She could make you do things. Just when you knew where you were, she could make you doubt yourself.

As we hurried up the gallery steps in the rain I could see Helen standing just inside the door, looking at her watch as if she'd never seen it before. Dardis rushed past her and then returned when she saw I'd stopped. She didn't wait to be intro-duced. "Don't look at Dennis that way. It's all my fault. We were almost here when I dragged him off the train." Helen's eyes glazed warily, but Dardis didn't notice, or pretended not to. She linked Helen's reluctant arm with her sisterly own. "You'll have to explain everything to us. Dennis and I are absolute Philistines when it comes to art." Helen detached herself and gave me a look.

The next two hours were no more successful. Dardis spent the first one wedged between Helen and myself, and the next lingering in tearful silence over a painting of beflowered Ophelia submerged in her orphaned grief. Helen, who was supposed to go back to the flat with us for dinner, pleaded a headache and suggested, while Dardis was buying a print of the Ophelia, that I go to her flat alone the next night. I could have gone. I was supposed to bring Dardis to Ulrich Seasley's house the next night, but that was not until nine. I hesitated, watching Dardis try to translate pounds and pence into dollars and cents. "Some other time then," Helen said. She did not wait to say good-bye to my sister.

On Sunday, Dardis wanted to go to church, so I took her to St. Paul's, but every hymn made her cry and we left long before the service was over. The sun had come out while we were inside and Dardis brightened in the fresh air. We walked for an hour or two in St. James's Park, without saying much. Then, while we leaned over a railing of one of the toy bridges in the park, watching the swans glide by, Dardis put her hand on my arm. "We'll get through, Denny. We'll help each other."

"Yes," I said, touched by her use of my old nickname. But I thought then that she was the one who needed all the help.

"And I think I'll stay away from church."

"Probably a good idea," I agreed.

That night after dinner we made our way through a maze of Victorian brick villas to Ulrich Seasley's house in Lancaster Gate. I had known Ulrich briefly and not very happily at

Chicago, where he'd held a visiting chair during my senior year and I'd been assigned to him to do odd jobs to help out his regular graduate assistant. He had been less than satisfied with my assistance, but when I ran into him that Friday at the top of the Holborn escalators he insisted that we must get together, must catch up.

"Come Sunday," he said. "Come for dinner. Well, dinner is a bit of a fuss, isn't it? Come for coffee. Nine?" I told him by way of an excuse that I had a visiting sister from America. "Of course you do," he said. "Of course. By all means."

This was 1973, the year not only of the worldwide oil crisis and gasoline shortage, but of a protracted coal miner's strike in England which resulted in drastic cutbacks: a three-day work week, electricity rationing, dark streets and buildings. The Seasleys' house was aglow with candles burning in the windows. Dardis was charmed by it, by the second-floor sitting room (we'd been gestured up the stairs by a sullen teenager with a half-shaved head), by the velvet drapes, which at least gave the impression of warmth, by Ulrich, lean and academic in a worn gray cardigan, by Janet with her long wine-colored skirt, frazzled hair, and the alert expression that comes from being cold all of the time. Ulrich was playing something vaguely recognizable on the violin while Janet accompanied him on the piano. Dardis squeezed my arm.

"How perfect," she whispered.

She advanced to take both of Janet's hands in both of hers, a gesture she had acquired, no doubt, from her recent experience with undertakers. Ulrich switched on a very small electric lamp and rubbed his hands together fussily. "I'm afraid you've come to us at a bad time," he said to Dardis. "You don't see us in our best light, so to speak."

"It's not nearly as bad here as it is at home," Dardis said. "People running over each other at gas stations, truckers shooting at each other on the Jersey Turnpike. At least you're civilized about it all."

"Yes, well." Annoyed that his joke had gone unnoticed, Ulrich adjusted the position of the lamp an inch. "Still, this strike *is* a dreadful nuisance."

"It's not really a strike," Dardis said. "We heard a man giving a speech on it in Hyde Park today. The miners are just refusing to work overtime until they're paid to work overtime. And you can see how much overtime they must usually work, if not doing it cripples the whole country. Do you know they're not even paid for the time it takes them to ride back up to the surface? I think they're absolutely right to strike. Or whatever they're doing."

"Do sit down," Ulrich said. "I'll just go and see about that coffee."

But Janet rematerialized just then with a tray and settled herself on the floor to pour. Dardis seemed to be considering the floor herself, so I patted the sofa next to me. Ulrich and I reminisced, carefully skirting all the points at which our paths had crossed. Janet looked at Ulrich. "I wish I could have been with you," she said. "But the children needed to be fed and looked after. And I'm afraid they were no comfort to me in your absence. They were all going through such difficult phases."

"That's the trouble with the moderns." Ulrich shook his head sadly. "They're always going through difficult phases. It's because they lack incentive, not to mention linguistic skills. Every allusion is lost on them. They understand nothing. No one has any Hebrew anymore. Even Latin and Greek are falling to the wayside."

"I'm going to learn German," Dardis announced. "Dennis promised to take me skiing in Austria for Christmas if I can learn how to order my own beer by then."

"Good for you." Ulrich smiled dismissively. "Good for you."

Then he turned his profile to her and Dardis sank into wounded silence until the "Irish problem" came up. Ulrich withdrew into the complicated history of Northern Ireland, but Janet waved an ascetic hand.

"The *real* problem is that the Catholics are so, well, so prolific. They've all got ten and twelve children each and can't feed or house or school them properly. And the Protestants, who do not procreate at such an alarming rate, are intimidated by their sheer numbers." She sipped her coffee thoughtfully. "What do you Americans think of it all?"

I could feel Dardis rekindling beside me and tried to set the tone by making a few cautious, noncommittal statements. Dardis set down her cup. "Why Dennis, you pompous ass. You know perfectly well that absolutely everybody thinks the problem would solve itself if the British would just get out of Ireland. The Protestants too, if they're so afraid of Catholics. They should go back to where they came from. I'm sure there's plenty of room in Scotland."

"My dear child." Janet's voice was as sharp as a governess's. "The Protestants have been in Ireland just as long as your people have been in America. Do you think that you should go back to where you came from and leave the country to the natives?"

"I already have." Dardis smiled her smile. "I mean, here I am."

HER TRUNKS ARRIVED TWO days later, just as she was coming in from her German class, three large steamer trunks we distributed inconveniently around the flat. They contained nearly everything she owned and Dardis was absorbed well into the night sorting through them. I watched her with growing irritation and diminishing comprehension. What did she think she was doing moving in on me like that, taking up all my space and fouling up my air with her cigarettes?

One trunk was full of books, which really annoyed me. I pointed out that London had the largest concentration of books in the world, but Dardis said she had to read her own copies. She had suddenly become very sentimental about objects. She slipped a tarnished brass candlestick from the sleeve of a bulky sweater and unwrapped a three-legged green cake plate from a moth-holed shawl that had been knitted by our grandmother before Dardis was born. I just looked at her.

"How can we have birthdays," she asked, reasonably, "without our birthday plate?" And then, like a cake, her bright face fell. I left her there and went to bed.

Helen was right, it seemed. The German was just what Dardis needed to keep her mind off things. The class met five mornings a week for three hours. It took her an hour to get there and another hour to get home. That was five hours spoken for right there. And then she had to work hard at it, memorizing vocabulary and idioms and dialogues. For the first couple of weeks, before she fell in with Alec, she was always at it when I came home.

But even then I think her interest was more in the class than in the language. Dardis was used to homogeneous college classrooms and she was surprised to find herself the youngest and most provincial of a cosmopolitan group.

"There's Herr Briggs, who's something in an embassy. He has a thing for Fräulein Morton, who translates children's fairy tales and looks like a prison matron. There's a Greek exile named Tennessee, who supports himself by importing backgammon boards and is writing a book on the game of chance. I asked him how he got his name and he said that his parents had gone to see *A Streetcar Named Desire* the night he was born. And there's a broody Sudanese who never speaks to anyone. He wears these strange ivy league clothes, tennis sweaters and things, but looks like he might have his pockets stuffed with hand grenades. Then there's a very haughty woman from Brazil, an opera singer I was told. She speaks English just like an American."

We were getting dinner ready, or rather Dardis was. I had told her there was no reason we shouldn't continue eating out, but she said it was a waste of money and, besides, she liked cooking. It made her feel at home. But shopping—she was already saying "marketing"—she found a mystery.

"I'm sure everything is here, if I can only crack the code. Dishwashing detergent is washing-up fluid. Cookies are biscuits. Biscuits are pastries. Pastries are tea cakes, and catsup is tomato sauce. But what is tomato sauce? If you were a can of tomato sauce, what would you call yourself? I kept asking for it and describing it and people kept handing me bottles of catsup. It would say Tomato Sauce on the label, but it would be a bottle of catsup. And ground beef, my God! This butcher was so rude to me today when I asked for ground beef. Turns out it's called minced meat. I thought minced meat was what you put into a mince pie. No?"

I drained the spaghetti while Dardis clucked over the watery sauce. At dinner she asked me if the name Alec Aire meant anything to me. It did not.

"He says he's an actor," she said. "He's going to bring me his clippings. Says he's Irish too, but he doesn't sound Irish. Sounds veddy veddy British."

"He must be Anglo Irish," I said. But Dardis gave me a blank look. She didn't know a thing about Ireland, and thinking about the scene she'd made at the Seasleys' made me want to strangle her.

"He must be very rich. You should see his clothes. But then, everybody in the class really *dresses*. I'm going to have to get some clothes."

"What's wrong with your clothes?" I gestured at the nearest steamer trunk.

"I wish you wouldn't do that, point with your fork. They're too young, that's what's wrong with them. And I need a haircut."

"Leave your hair alone. You look fine." She did. Her hair straight and black and swinging around her shoulders when she turned her head. Her eyes, my mother's eyes, the color of wisteria.

"But other people look older than I do. Alec wears these dark three-piece suits and a cashmere overcoat. Silk scarf, beautiful shoes. All black. He says you can't wear brown shoes in the city."

"Of course you can. I do."

"Yes." She looked at me critically. "But Alec is full of opinions. He says I can't seriously call myself Dardis. He says it's a man's name."

"It is not. It's your name."

"That's exactly what I said, but he just rolled his eyes. He has very nice eyes. He's quite good-looking, in a theatrical way. And very odd. You know, eccentric. He carries an attaché case and unpacks it as soon as he comes in, which is always almost an hour late: a stack of good paper, a fountain pen, a bottle of ink. But he never takes any notes. He just chain smokes, these fat little cigarettes that come in an orange box. They're very good. He gave me one today. Right in the middle of a dialogue, he leaned across the table and offered me one. 'Try one of these,' he said. 'Those Marlboros are filthy.' He didn't even lower his voice. He's very disruptive. Makes a big production out of coming in late, closing the door, hanging up his coat, unpacking his attaché case. He hates the class, hates the instructor, hates German."

"Then why is he taking it?"

"He says he's always being asked to play Germans and wants to do it authentically. But he says it's an ugly language and that the only thing you can say in it is that if you have lots of money you will have no spare time, and if you have lots of spare time you will have no money."

"Goethe," I said. "Nietzsche, Heidegger, Heine. Mann."

"But listen to this." Dardis left the table and came back with a slim red volume. "This is the dialogue we did today. Herr Hartmann and his little secretary Fräulein Klein. Herr Hartmann has everything. He has ein house, ein gross house, he has zwei autos, tons of money, but no time to enjoy them. Er hat leider keine zeit. Fräulein Klein, on the other hand, has no house, no auto, no money. Aber she hat oodles of zeit." Dardis flipped through the pages. "There's nothing in here about how to rent a pair of skis."

THE FOLLOWING MONDAY THE flat was empty when I came in at six, which surprised me. Dardis was always there ahead of me. I poured myself a drink and checked the contents of my midget refrigerator: eggs, cream cheese, some withered vegetables, a few sausages. I cracked all of the eggs into a bowl, mashed the cream cheese with a fork, diced an onion, and put the sausages in a pan over a low flame. Then I set the table and sat down with a book to wait for Dardis. When she wasn't in by eight, I made an omelette big enough for three and ate it with the sausages.

At ten I got up to go meet Helen, who supplemented her instructor's salary by waiting on tables three nights a week in a Holborn restaurant. I put on my coat, then took it off again. I thought I ought to be there when the police came for me. Dardis still wasn't home when I went to bed at two, telling myself not to panic, Dardis wasn't a child. But she was, and I was just getting back up again when she came in, feeling no pain.

"You still up, Dennis?" She took off her coat and flung it. "I've had the most wonderful day. I had lunch with Alec."

"You had lunch? For fifteen hours?" I was angry with her for making me feel like a father.

"We had dinner too. Don't be such a snit. I couldn't very well let you know, could I?" One of the drawbacks of the flat was that there was no telephone. "Let's have a drink and I'll tell you."

"I'll tell you" was a phrase of hers. Give me those Superman comics and I'll tell you. Stay with me until I fall asleep and I'll tell you. Something she knew and you didn't: why Mrs. Bayliss was crying in the kitchen that morning; why Mr. Hanley was no longer teaching sixth grade; why Janice Tubert had stayed home. I reacted to it like a ten-year-old.

"You've had enough to drink, and I'm going back to bed." This time I shut the door, and locked it, which made me feel even sillier.

When I emerged in the morning Dardis was already in the kitchen, making coffee and nursing a hangover. "How could you be such a pig as to eat all those eggs and half a dozen sausages? I'm so hungry!" Dardis had a way of turning things around. I poured some coffee and took it into the dining room. She came in balancing a mug with a knife sticking out of it, a jar of marmalade and a box of soda crackers tucked under her arm. She sipped her coffee and make a sour face.

"Feeling a little under the weather, Dardis?"

"Lousy. My mouth tastes like a litter box." She spread four crackers with marmalade and ate them deliberately, medicinally. "I'm giving you notice, so you won't go all mother hen on me again. I won't be home for dinner tonight either. You can get Helen to feed you."

"I can feed myself." I refused to ask where she was going.

"Alec wants me to meet a friend of his," she volunteered. "He's coming down from Scotland today. We're going to talk him into joining the German class and I'm supposed to coach him, because Alec certainly can't. That's why he asked me to lunch yesterday."

"It took him long enough to ask."

"We went to Harrod's too, and lots of other places. He couldn't believe I hadn't been to Harrod's. Why didn't you take me?"

"It was on my list," I said. It was, in a way. Just days before, I'd asked Helen to take Dardis with her when she mentioned she was going to a sale at Harrod's the next morning. But she'd just said, "Don't, Dennis. Please, just don't."

"We spent two hours browsing in the food stalls alone. They have untold American goodies, even tomato sauce. They have actual mayonnaise, and canned pumpkin. I bought some to make us a pie for Thanksgiving, but I seem to have lost it. I should have had it delivered. Alec says Harrod's will deliver a match. He bought some chocolates and the clerk put them in a bag. But he said, 'None of your filthy plastic bags. Please box them properly,' so she boxed them and tied it with string and handed him the box. But he gave her his card and told her to send them."

"He sounds like a creep."

"But he's not. He's not. He was just playing Oscar Wilde. He told me some wonderful Oscar Wilde stories. One about Wilde sailing into Fortnam and Mason's and saying, 'I'll have those flowers out of your window, and this and that and those,' and when the clerk had gathered everything up and asked where to send them, he said, 'Oh, I don't *want* them. I merely thought they looked ghastly in your window,' and sailed out."

I just looked at her.

"Maybe I didn't tell it right. He really is very funny. He does Noel Coward too. He's always quoting him and singing snatches of his songs. He wants to do a show impersonating him, the way people do Mark Twain, and take it to America. That's what he calls it. He doesn't seem to know anything about the United States. You can tell by the questions he asks. One thing he asked me yesterday was: Who was the last king of America?" She got up and waltzed out to the kitchen, her robe billowing regally behind her, and came back with the coffeepot. I held out my cup.

"Who's the friend?"

"A Scottish earl, or the son of an earl. He'll be my second. I met one at dinner last night. He was with a friend of Alec's, an artist who designed a huge tapestry that's hanging in the Victoria and Albert or the War Museum or somewhere. I forget."

She told me how the earl had just finished turning his ancestral home into a sort of Disneyland for tourists, complete with moat rides for the kiddies. Her second earl, it seemed, was a young alcoholic. He had lived with Herr Aire until the previous spring when he went on a binge, drank a case of something and gambled away a fortune. His family, who had incarcerated him for six months, was about to turn him loose again and Alec, with what Dardis evidently took for commendable concern for his friend's welfare, wanted to get him involved in something right away.

"If he gets into trouble again his parents will cut him off." She spread another four crackers and ate them. "Alec thinks German will be just the thing, because he'll have to work so hard to catch up."

"What makes you think the dipso earl wants to learn German?"

"Because if he does," Dardis spread her hands reasonably, "Alec will take him skiing in Austria over Christmas."

"Forget it, Dardis." I pushed away from the table. "Don't even think about it." But she started to laugh. She was just seeing how far she could go. She ate another cracker, thoughtfully.

"He does want to meet you, though. He says you sound devoted."

"Do I?"

"But I don't think you two would hit it off," she said. "You're so different. You're such a proletarian, and he's an aristocrat. Oh, don't look so wounded, Dennis. You *are* a worker bee, and he's a queen." She didn't know, I thought, how right she was. I raised my cup to her.

"If I'm a proletarian, what does that make you? I am your brother, you know."

"Oh, shut up."

"Your *devoted* brother. The one who's supposed to be taking care of you. So don't ever do that to me again. You scared the hell out of me last night."

"Just leave me alone, Dennis." She was actually angry; I couldn't believe it. "I can take care of myself."

That was Dardis all over. You don't ask her to come. In fact, you ask her not to come. But she says she's a basket case, she needs you. So you let her come, let her move in, let her make you play house. Then, when you worry because she stays out all night, she's suddenly made a complete recovery. She can take care of herself.

"You do that," I said. "I have other things to do."

I DID HAVE A lot of work to do. My field exams were coming up in December and I'd let things slide since Dardis arrived. There was Helen too, and it hadn't been possible to be with both Helen and Dardis at the same time. I still saw Helen at LSE, still had lunch with her more often than not, still met her after work a couple of nights a week, walked her home, still stayed over occasionally. But not nearly as often, because I didn't want to leave Dardis alone. So I was glad Dardis had met someone, anyone, to take her off my hands. Her lunches and dinners continued to go far into the night and we began communicating through the notes we'd tape to the bathroom mirror: "We're out of coffee." "These towels are filthy; your turn."

But from time to time she'd get up when I was going out, or I'd get up when she was coming in, and we'd talk. She'd fill me in. Malcolm, the friend, was incredibly handsome, the kind of man Shakespeare would have written sonnets to, and brilliant: he was catching up; Dardis was tutoring him in his flat while Alec brooded watchfully in a corner; he was caught up; he was turning star pupil. Then Malcolm, the ex-friend, was a degenerate ingrate; he was taking up with Tennessee; he was drinking again; he and the Greek were dropping out of the German class; he was moving out of Alec's flat.

Dardis's affection for Alec seemed to increase with his disappointments. She was always trying to think of ways to cheer him up, always buying him presents. He loved presents, she said. She even bought him an expensive silk shirt because he preferred silk next to his skin. If he ever gave her anything, she never mentioned it. I was more than curious about the nature of their relationship, but didn't ask questions. Whatever it was, Dardis was already off and running; it was just a matter of when she would fall on her face.

And I was, I must admit, almost looking forward to that. Whenever she looked at me now it was with an appraising, critical eye. Her accent was changing daily. She'd acquired a whole arsenal of unfamiliar gestures as well as a new wardrobe and vocabulary. She'd cut her hair, too short, and the champion of Irish Catholic mothers and underpaid coal miners was now saying things like, "I don't know why people bother having second sons. They can't *do* anything for them." Her friend Alec, it seemed, was a second son. One afternoon I came in and found her standing by the window, elocuting: "Ye mariners of England, who guard our native seas . . ."

"Practicing your German, Dardis?" I knew she didn't go to

the Goethe Institute anymore. She and Alec had dropped out
on the heels of the other two.

"My vowels. Alec gave me this poem to learn. He says that
when you can recite it properly you can speak English properly.
It has every vowel sound in it. He gives speech lessons whenever he's really broke."

"How much is he charging you?"

Part of my irritation with the new Dardis was the old competition. She'd always been able to reach into any grab bag
blindfolded and come up with the grand prize. She had a way of
finding whatever was to be found anywhere. When we'd go
beachcombing on summer vacations, she'd find ten-dollar bills
and gold rings; I'd find punctured condoms and bent tampons.
I didn't particularly envy her her new friends. They sounded like
a bad lot to me. On the other hand, I hadn't come across any
earls, or even a phony countess.

She told me one morning she'd had a row with a countess
the night before. "Well, it wasn't really a row, and she's not
really a countess. She just calls herself one because her last husband was an Italian. She got very nasty when this perfectly nice
man she was with got drunk and started pouring himself all over
me. She told Alec to take me home. She said she was sure it was
past my bedtime."

"And did he?"

"No. I had to walk for an hour trying to get a cab. With all
the lights out, it was terrifying."

When I told Helen that one, she turned on me. "I don't
understand you, Dennis. What *can* you mean, letting your sister
fall in with that fat lot of phonies? It will take her years to get
her head right again. You should send her straight home. Now."

"Let her? Send her? Dardis?" I had to laugh. "Anyway,
there's no place to send her. She dropped out of school, she
rented out the house."

"Isn't there anyone else? Grandparents? Uncles, aunts, cousins?"

"No," I said. "There's no one but us."

She raised her eyebrows warily. "Us?"

"Dardis and me."

BUT I DIDN'T EVEN remember her birthday. I knew Dardis's birthday came a week or so after Thanksgiving, but Thanksgiving had come and gone unnoticed, and neither of us mentioned Christmas anymore. Besides, I was working fourteen hours a day for my exams. There was some talk of birthdays on the last morning of my exams, Alec's birthday. Dardis told me she'd given him an old George and Ira Gershwin record that Alec played over and over until Jack, his valet, who Dardis said hated Americans and especially her, broke it in half.

"But he already knew it by heart," she said. "He closed Paulette's every night singing 'My Cousin from Milwaukee.'" I was shaving and she was sitting on the edge of the tub watching, waiting for me to finish so she could have a bath; I was too distracted to note her use of the past tense.

"What's Paulette's?" I asked her.

"It's a place in Chelsea, a sort of restaurant. Alec always wanted to go there because he's looking for work and lots of theatre people hang out there. Lots of homosexuals, too," she added. "But not the kind Mommy used to hang around with." I caught her eye in the mirror.

"*Hang around?*"

"Well, she did. Stephen was her closest friend, wasn't he?"

"They worked together, Dardis. He was a serious person. Your mother was a serious person."

She got up and walked out. I reached over and turned off the faucet in the bathtub, which already had a foot of water in it. When I came out, Dardis was standing in the kitchen doorway. "Let's have breakfast. I'll cook something."

"I can't." I put on my coat. "I'll get some coffee on the way. I need to look over my notes. Today," I announced, on my way out the door, "happens to be the last day of my field exams."

"Oh," she said, surprised. "Well, good luck."

When I came in that afternoon she was there, wearing something new, something dark and sophisticated, and the floor was littered with shopping bags and boxes.

"Oh, good." She spun around to be admired. "You're here."

"Not for long," I said. "Helen and I are going to see *Savages*. I just came in to change."

"The new Paul Scofield? I've been wanting to see that. Maybe I could come with you."

"Sorry," I said. "Sold out."

"Why don't you bring Helen back here, after? I've got some—"

"How can I bring anyone back here," I interrupted. "With you camping out all over the place?" I shoved a shoe box aside with my foot. "What is all this?" She was hurt, but she slapped on a hat of Picasso blue and shot me an alarming look.

"Do you know your Dos Passos? 'Faulty costuming makes role of fierce warrior difficult to play.' Or something like that."

"Who are you planning to slay? The queen bee?"

She didn't answer, so I went to shower and change. When I came out she had managed to stash everything somewhere and was sitting in an armchair, looking depressed. "Do you have time for a drink with me before you go?"

"Just." I poured a small whiskey for me and a large one for Dardis. "Where's all your upper-crust friends tonight?"

"Oh, I don't know." She patted the arm of her chair, but I remained standing. "Anyway, how were your exams? Are you really finished now?"

"I'm finished with the exams. Next year is all donkey work. This was the last big hurdle. It went pretty well. I think I did all right."

"I'm so glad." She smiled up at me. "Dennis, why didn't you tell me?"

"I didn't think you'd be interested in anything so prole-tarian as exams." It was true, but it came out sounding a lot more sarcastic than I'd intended. She flushed and looked away.

"You'd better go. You'll be late."

I was in the mood to celebrate that night. The fact was I'd been pretty worried about my exams and I knew I'd done much better than just all right on them. I wanted champagne. But Helen didn't drink at all, so after the theatre we went for coffee instead. I drank three cups, which gave me the shakes, and lis-tened to Helen poke holes in the play, which I had really enjoyed but she thought a facile treatment of a serious subject. I tried to return the ball once in a while, but my heart wasn't in it. I kept seeing Dardis slap on that hat. I kept wishing she had come with us. Helen never mentioned my exams except for an oblique reference when she pushed back her chair to leave: "You must be exhausted. I know *I* am."

IT WASN'T EVEN TWELVE when I got home. Dardis was sitting at my desk, writing a letter, a twenty-pager, from the looks of it. I took out my disappointment on her. "Poor Cinderella. No last-minute invitation to the ball?"

Dardis looked up at the clock. "Poor Dennis. Afraid you'll turn into a pumpkin?"

"Yes," I said. "Something like that." I went into my room and took off my coat and tie, pulled on a sweater, then came out again. I regretted that crack about her camping out. At this moment, I really was glad she was there.

"I'm going to have a drink. Want one?"

Dardis put down her pen and swung around from the desk. "Yum, I said, yum, I will, yum." Dardis was one in a million.

"You're a rare girl, Dardis."

"Woman," she said, getting up and tucking her hair behind her ears. "I'm a woman. I'm twenty-two years old. Today."

I just looked at her. Her navy blue robe made of towel, her shiny black hair cut short and turning away from her cheeks, her long nose peaked and her long toes pinked from the cold. My throat closed. Dardis managed a smile.

"Don't look so stricken." She thrust her hands deep into the pockets of her robe. "I haven't been exactly thoughtful myself."

"Look," I said. "Get dressed. It's not too late. We'll go out. We'll celebrate. Champagne, whatever you want."

"I've already got champagne, two bottles. I bought them this morning when you told me about your exams. I thought you might need them, whichever way they went." I followed her out to the kitchen and put my hand on her shoulder, turned her around. Her eyes were bright, too bright.

"Happy Birthday, Bird."

It was my father's pet name for her, because of her beaky nose, and apparently the wrong thing to say. It triggered the flood the bright eyes had threatened. She put her arms around me and I patted her awkwardly, afraid of her tears. She cried and cried, whole months, years of tears, rocking us from side to side, dangerously sucking me into the whirlpool of her grief. Finally I disentangled myself and put her self-consciously away from me. I tore off a paper towel from the rack and handed it to her.

Gradually, she stopped crying. She blew her nose and stood at the sink, splashing cold water on her face, while I moved restlessly around the kitchen, opening drawers at random, shutting them again. Then Dardis opened the refrigerator, took out a bottle of champagne and tossed it to me. I opened it, letting the cork plunge into the false pasteboard ceiling put in by the schoolteachers to conserve heat. Dardis took two glasses from the shelf, new ones, and held them up to catch the light. They looked familiar.

"Did you bring them from home?"

"No. I bought them today, but they're the same pattern. I'm going to leave them with you." Her voice was nasal, uneven. "The candlesticks too. And the cake plate, after we eat the cake I bought." I followed her into the sitting room and fell into a chair across from her.

"What do you mean, leave them?"

"I'm going back. After Christmas, that is. I'm not ready to face that alone yet. I don't care whether we go to Austria or not, but I'm going to spend Christmas with you. Then I'm leaving. I made my reservations this afternoon."

"Don't go. I didn't mean what I said this afternoon, about camping out."

"Yes, you did. But if it was anything you said, it was what you said this morning, about my not being a serious person."

"I didn't say that."

"You implied it."

"I wasn't talking about you. I meant your friend Herr Aire." Dardis just cocked her head to the side and looked at me.

"Okay," I said. "I was talking about you. I'm sorry."

She shook her head, no, then asked, suddenly, "Will you be coming home for the summer?" I didn't answer right away. I didn't know what to say. I hadn't been home for the summer in years. She shook her head again. "Never mind." Then she covered her eyes with a hand and started to cry again. I realized that this was more than I'd thought. I went and crouched by her chair.

"What's the matter? Did something happen?" She cried harder for a minute and then stopped, blew her nose again.

"Something did happen. But it's not that."

"What?" I was visited by the image of her wandering the dark streets of London alone, at two o'clock in the morning. "What happened?"

"I don't want to talk about it. Not now. I can't. Besides, it's not that. I told you."

"Then what is it?"

"I'm just so—" She left a pause. "Afraid."

"Of what?"

"I don't know. Everything." She blew her nose again. "I'm supposed to be twenty-two years old, but I feel like I'm ten. I'm just not ready." She sighed, took a deep breath, then a long drink of champagne. "I'm all right. I'll be all right. Hand me that ashtray, will you?" I did, and then returned to my chair.

"Look. Don't go back," I said. "Stay here. You can go to school here or something."

"No. I haven't burned all my bridges. I can go back in January. I won't graduate in May. But that's just as well. It'll give me more time to think, to make some decisions. I'll get a job for the summer. Or maybe I'll take some courses. I don't know." She passed a hand over her eyes and I was afraid she was going to cry again, but she lit a cigarette instead. When she spoke her voice was a lot more steady, in control.

"I'm on my own, Dennis. I just realized that today, when nobody remembered my birthday. I realized there's nobody to answer to now except myself. So I better start asking some questions."

"You've still got me." I reached over and refilled her glass, then mine. "We're orphans, remember? We have to stick together."

"Do I? Do I really have you?" She looked at me. "You've been nice and polite to me, because you're a nice and polite person. But I wonder sometimes if you really care about me. I wonder if, deep down, you really wish me well."

"How can you say that?" I was hurt, but I also knew it was true that I had been looking forward to seeing her fall on her face.

"Am I wrong? I hope so, Dennis, because I really love you. But I was thinking today, I was wondering if you always forget my birthday because subconsciously you wish I'd never been born."

"That's ridiculous, Dardis. That's stupid talk. You've been reading too much pop psychology."

"I haven't been reading anything," she said, sharply. "I've been thinking, about you and me, about how different we are." She waited a while. "I need so much, and you need so little. You need so little," she added, "you can get it from almost anyone. You can get it from Helen."

"That's not fair."

"No, it's not *fair*." She smiled at my instinctive childish response. "But it's how we turned out. I'm an emotional Ferris wheel, and you don't let anything touch you. You didn't even cry at Mommy and Daddy's funerals, not once."

"Maybe that's because you cried enough for ten people. Somebody had to hold you up."

"That's what I've been thinking about." She nodded sadly. "I've been wondering if I might have robbed you of your emotions." I was really angry now. I started to get up, but she swung her bare feet up into my lap, as if to pin me down. She put out a hand. "Wait. Let me finish. Please?" But she lit a cigarette and smoked in silence for a few minutes.

"Do you remember the time we almost drowned?" she said, at last.

"No." But then, all at once, I did: her fat little arms strangling me, her knees battering me in the stomach, the groin; the light slipping away.

"Yes you do. We were at that lake. Mommy and Daddy

were lying on a blanket and we were in the water. We were playing on that slide. It was one of those double slides with one ladder. When you got to the top you could either go down the short chute into the shallow water or the long one into the deep water. We went down the short one over and over. You'd sit behind me and wrap your legs around me and we'd go down screaming. Then I wanted to try the long slide. The water was way over our heads and I couldn't swim. I nearly drowned you, but you didn't let me go. We went down and up, down and up. It seemed like years. Then the lifeguard pulled us out. First he yelled at you for taking me out there, then when Mommy and Daddy got there they yelled at you for not taking care of me."

"It could have been worse," I said. "I could have let you drown. Then they'd really have been mad."

"You were only nine years old, Dennis. You were nine years old and nearly drowned and no one comforted you. I got held and patted and fussed over, and you were ignored. Worse, you were punished. I can't get that picture out of my mind, you standing there all blue and cold and shivering. You were crying too, but no one paid any attention to you."

Dardis went on talking for a long time, about how representative of our childhoods that incident was, how she'd been spoiled as a result and had come to always expect the lion's share of whatever was going around, while I'd learned not to look for much, in an emotional way. I was listening, thinking, looking down absently at my sister's long toes, when I remembered something, saw it with such clarity that I took hold of her feet and held on to them.

That same night, at the lake. There was an amusement park nearby, but Dardis and I, having had our share of adventure for the day, refused even the merry-go-round. Our parents—still in love, I saw now—parked us on a bench and went to ride the

Ferris wheel. Dardis slumped against my shoulder and went to sleep while I watched, awed and terrified, as our parents, their arms around each other, swung suddenly up and away from us, laughing, as they disappeared backwards into the night.

The One with the Heart

Michelle got her job through Mr. Blancharde, who was the credit manager and played tennis with her father, so she resented the changes at Robertson's even more than I did, although I had worked there longer. I started as a sales clerk in the men's department the summer I finished high school. I thought I was going to school in Boston in the fall. I thought that's what I was saving money for.

Department stores had a different sound then, cash register drawers binging open and sales slips whooshing through pneumatic tubes overhead. When you charged something the clerk would roll up the sales slip and tuck it into a glass cylinder, the kind they have at the outer stations of drive-in banks now. She'd slide the cylinder into one of the tubes and press a button. A bell would ring, a dull gong, and the cylinder would shoot up five floors to the credit department where they'd check your account, initial the sales slip and send it back down. Then you'd get your package. But most people had everything delivered, those distinctive dark green trucks going out at the end of every morning and afternoon. There was a different smell, too, a combination of permanent-wave lotion and blue rinse sent off by the elderly women in white gloves who drifted down the escalators all day from the beauty salon, their hair cloudy and stiff as Brillo pads.

Robertson's was already making some changes that first
summer. Mr. Robertson, grandson of the original, still came
through regularly, greeting employees by name, asking after
husbands, wives, children, parents, grandparents. And one wall
of Notions was still hung with the sepia prints that showed the
store's first customers emerging from their carriages under the
porte cochere at the Main Street entrance. But the pneumatic
tubes were being replaced by air-conditioning ducts, and telephones were installed in every department so charges could
be authorized more quickly. A bank of twenty telephones was
added to the credit office, so that the adjacent book department
had to be shunted down to the first floor.

Changes were taking place at home too. That was the
summer my father had his first massive coronary, and the
summer my mother discovered, too late, a lump in her breast. I
was the last one home and did not go away to school that fall,
after all, but enrolled in the local university, which I'd always
thought of as a place where you got your teeth cleaned by dental
students for fifty cents, and I applied for a better-paying job in
the newly expanded credit department at Robertson's, filing
sales slips and answering the twenty telephones strung out along
the customer files. I worked there several nights a week, Satur-
days, summers, semester breaks, reading in the employees' cafeteria, reading in the hospital waiting room, reading in line at the
grocery store, reading at the dinner table.

Michelle, who went to school in Washington, came to
work in the credit department during her Christmas break. I'd
never met her before, although we were almost the same age
and in the winter could actually see each other's houses from
our bedroom windows. She lived just across the Colonial
Parkway from me, but in a different world. Her parents were
young and healthy. Mine were old and not. Before the coronary
and the cancer, there had been trouble with kidneys and gall

bladders, operations, complications. Michelle's parents played tennis and golf, swam and went to dances at the country club. They gave parties and had a teakwood bar at one end of their Polynesian sun porch. They called each other darling. They called me darling. They insisted I call them Sophie and Chad, which I had trouble with at first. I could not imagine Michelle addressing my parents as Joan and Walter. I could not imagine them saying to her, "Michelle, darling. Can I fix you a drink?"

SHORTLY AFTER HE HIRED Michelle, Mr. Blancharde, who'd been the credit manager all my life, lost his own job. Mr. Robertson died and his daughters sold out to a chain, who right away opened up two branch stores in suburban shopping malls. They dismantled the porte cochere at the main entrance, took down the sepia prints of the store's first customers, reorganized department after department, and sent in a team of efficiency experts to overhaul the credit operation. The first thing they did there was to replace Mr. Blancharde with a much younger man. They didn't fire Mr. Blancharde, or pension him off. They moved him out of his big office with a wall of windows overlooking the downtown park, to a small desk just outside what had been his office, where his new job was to place threatening phone calls to customers, most of whom he knew, and demand immediate payment on delinquent accounts. He was dead in six months.

Michelle and I could not forgive the new man for that, even though none of the fatal decisions had been his, even though he had always treated Mr. Blancharde with respect. We didn't speak to Mark McCloud unless we had to. We received his instructions in silence and when we had to get his approval for a charge on an overextended account, we would hand him the file and take it back without a word. He weathered our hostility with the same good grace that soon won over everyone else in the department, including Kate Coyle, who was sixty-one, had worked at Robertson's since she was twelve, had presided over Authorizing for thirty years, and had called Mr. Blancharde "Robert." Mr. McCloud treated us with a detached amusement I secretly approved of, but I didn't want to give in before Michelle did. I was completely in her sway. I held out all through the summer, right up until she went back to school in September. So she was surprised, when she came back at Christmas, to find us sitting together in the employees' cafeteria, drinking coffee and laughing.

JENNY HILL WAS ANOTHER girl who dazzled me, but in a different way from Michelle, who had silky black hair, bright blue eyes, and the faintest, palest sprinkle of freckles across a small, perfect nose. Jenny and I had worked together for a few weeks in Men's before she was transferred to Ladies' Lingerie. She was tall and pencil-slim with sleek dark hair she wore cut short and tucked behind her ears to frame elaborate earrings. She had high cheekbones and fine features and was always tanned by the first of June. Michelle and I wore flat shoes and shirtwaist dresses, but Jenny wore stiletto heels and silk shirts, dark skirts so narrow she could not walk up stairs and had to stand perfectly still on the escalators, except for raising a pair of lovely bare arms to smooth her flawless hair. She liked to shock people. She told me once that she and her sister wore nothing but underwear around the house in the summer, and that their father would slap them and scream at them to put some clothes on.

We had never been friends, and she hardly ever spoke to me once she no longer had to. Until Mark McCloud took over the credit department. Then she started "dropping by to say hello," which meant taking the escalators or elevator all the way up to the sixth floor, where she'd lean over the customer service

counter yoo-hooing for me so that he would hear and look up.
She was always something to see. She made a point now too of
looking for me in the cafeteria. This particular day she'd been
on her way out when she spotted me and Mr. McCloud at a
table near the door and came over. I would have introduced her,
but she started talking immediately.

"You wouldn't believe this guy this morning, Marge." No
one else ever called me Marge, a name I've always hated. "He
wants to buy a bra for his wife. So I have to ask him her size,
right? He says he doesn't know her size, but he can describe her.
So he starts describing her, moving his hands. Melons, he says,
cantaloupes, big scoops of vanilla ice cream. The guy was nuts.
I had to call the store detective."

She kept glancing at Mr. McCloud, but he was concen-
trating on his coffee, hunching over it the way a very tall person
sometimes does, and he never really looked up until she was
gone, when he looked at me over his coffee cup and smiled.
Then he started to laugh. He laughed until the tears came. He
was laughing, and I was laughing, when Michelle came in,
loaded with packages. She stopped just inside the door and
stood there a lot longer than was necessary.

When she came over, Mr. McCloud got up and pulled out
a chair for her. She dropped her packages on it, but remained
standing. Her packages were mostly from other stores and he
asked her if she was going over to the enemy. Her eyes swept
over him, but it was to me she spoke, saying how she'd spent the
entire morning Christmas shopping with her mother, buying all
the presents her mother thought she should buy for people. "I'm
completely broke now," she said. "But when I told her I could
not write one more check, she thought I was just too tired."

Mr. McCloud saw that she wouldn't sit down until he left,
so he looked at his watch and got up. She sat in his chair and
watched him go, raised an eyebrow. "Well, you two looked very

cozy, you and Mr. McCloudy." This was another thing she dis-
approved of, the way he spelled his name. He was part of the
Macleod family of Indian Neck, but had changed his name to
a more phonetic spelling when he enlisted in the navy after
some trouble with his family. We'd heard all this from
Michelle's parents.

"That was just because of Jenny Hill," I said, and described
the scene. She put her elbows on the table, framed her face with
cupped hands and looked at me with her blue eyes.

"But why on earth were you sitting together in the first
place?"

"I was sitting here first. He stopped by to ask if I'd work a
few extra nights a week until Christmas."

"How many nights?" Her black lashes came down a notch.
"Three."

"That's in addition to your usual three? So you're working
every night."

She sniffed, and took out her enameled cigarette case. "I
wonder why he didn't ask me to work any extra nights. I wrote
and asked him for extra nights, and God knows I need the
money as much as you do. Why do you suppose he asked you,
and not me?" She lit her cigarette and raised both eyebrows.

BUT IT WAS A couple of months more before I began running
into Mark McCloud in too many places too many times for
mere coincidence. I got tired of the cafeteria menu cycle and
started walking four blocks to a diner where no one from the
store ever ate. Then he started going there. He didn't sit with
me at first. But after a few times he did. He would come in usually just after my food arrived. I would always leave as soon as I
was finished and go find someplace else to read. It wasn't that I
disliked him or that he bothered me. I didn't. He didn't. It was
just that I had all this reading to do.

Then he started taking courses at the university and I would run into him between classes. He was always standing outside a classroom, as if he were waiting for it to empty out, as if he had a class there next. But this was the liberal arts building. I knew he didn't have any classes there. We'd just say hello. I never stopped to talk. Then he started going to the bar just off campus where some of the English majors went after classes. He would sit at the bar and drink a beer, and then leave. He'd raise a hand sometimes, say hello, but never joined us. I never asked him to. The booth was always full, and we were talking Transcendentalism and Naturalism. He was in Business. Besides, I was in love with somebody else.

It's only in the rearview mirror that I can see Mark McCloud with any clarity at all. (I dreamed about him recently, twenty-some years later, which is what made me remember all this.) At the time he was totally eclipsed by Alfred, a blue-eyed, flaxen-haired young Werther. He was eclipsed first by Alfred's presence, and then by his absence.

The Sorrows of Young Werther was just one of the things Alfred gave me to read. There were also the Brownings' collected letters, the collected works of Thomas Mann and Thomas Hardy, lots of poetry, lots of plays. All of this would have been fine, if I didn't already have too much to read. That year I was supposed to be reading all of Shakespeare and Milton and Spenser, Emerson, Thoreau, Whitman, Melville. But Alfred would leave things on my doorstep, sometime during the night, or when I wasn't home, and I would read them right away, right through, all night, looking for a message. He would waylay me in the parking lot when I was getting into my car to go to the hospital and take me instead to New Haven or Hartford or to a roadhouse near the New York state line. He would show me pieces of poetry he'd been writing himself and for weeks I would wonder, Whose black velvet ribbon? Whose Alpine pillow? I found out whose after more than a year of this when he left without warning, without even saying good-bye, for Switzerland, where it turned out he had a wife and three-year-old daughter. He told me in a letter that came a month after he disappeared.

After that I stopped going to the bar off campus and took to walking the beach every day after classes. Five miles out, five miles back. I never saw anything the whole way. Then I started seeing Mark McCloud's car parked up on the road near the end of the beach. After three or four times, I was annoyed. I wanted to say, "What are you doing here? Leave me alone." But he was asleep, sound asleep behind the wheel with a Management textbook open in his lap. The windows were rolled up tight and I rapped on the passenger window. He half opened one eye, but I don't think he saw me. I don't think he woke up. I remember walking away, thinking, I hope to God I never get to the point where I need sleep that badly, where I have to take a nap.

He wasn't that much older than I was, but he had all these kids, little ones: one, two, three. I'd been to his house. I'd filled in for a babysitter who canceled one night when they had a wedding to go to. They lived in the next town and I thought he must have been desperate to ask me. They lived in one of those cramped saltbox houses with a patch of yard and a depressing wire fence around it. No trees, toys everywhere, a playpen in the middle of the living room.

He had been normal enough in the car, talking about work and school, but at home he was different. He was as sullen and silent as an adolescent, and this was a man who had a certain amount of stature in the workplace, authority and respect. He and his wife acted as if they hadn't been introduced yet. She was wearing a green taffeta dress with an apron over it, and too much makeup. She was trying to feed the baby, who was spitting spinach at her. "Here, let me do that," I said, just for something to say. I wished they would leave. I wished I could leave myself.

I don't mean that I felt sorry for him. I did not. I was still at the age when you believe that people get what they ask for. I believed, if I thought about it at all, that the life he and his wife lived together was what they must have had in mind from the very beginning, that if they suffered from anything it was from a failure of imagination. I didn't know then how those nightmare delivery-vans can sneak up on you when you aren't looking, and unload a lot of things you never ordered. Besides, I didn't have any sympathy to spare. I was using it all up on myself. He was the sympathetic one. He was the one with the heart.

IT WAS MARCH, I know, because it was eight months after Alfred disappeared and I had been counting. I went into the student center for a cup of coffee on a windy, rainy day, and there he was, Alfred, sitting at the same table where I'd first met him, wearing the same sweater that exactly matched his eyes. He lifted his hand in a casual way, as if we'd seen each other yesterday, or ten minutes ago, and said, "Can you loan me a dime for a cup of coffee?" which wasn't as cruel as it sounds, because it was what he'd said to me the first time I met him. I don't suppose he needed the dime this time. He just wanted credit for remembering.

My heart turned over at least twice. I thought he'd Come Back. But he cleared that up right away. He'd just come back to sell his little red TR IV, which had been draped in canvas all this time and parked next to Professor Scott's house where I could see it every day. He talked a lot, trying to explain things, telling me his story, how his wife had left him, taken the baby and gone back to Switzerland, where she was from, how he'd gone to pieces. I didn't say anything. I just kept stirring my coffee and watching our friends come in one after another, stop, then skirt the table at the last minute. At one point he wrote an address on a piece of paper and pushed it across the table. There was a phone number too. "This is where I work. If you ever get to Zurich . . ." Before he left, he said, "Don't judge me, Margaret. You don't know what it's like when someone leaves you that way, when the bottom suddenly drops out of your world."

He was right, of course. I didn't know that yet. I didn't know very much at all, except for a few irregular verbs. But I thought I did. Right then I thought I knew all there was to know.

I walked the beach every day, rain or shine. It rained a lot in March, but I let nothing deter me from my grief. Mark was there one day. I recognized him from a long way off, although he looked different in jeans and a black pullover. It must have been a Sunday. I'd never seen him in anything but a business suit. But his height, his gait, and the stoop of his shoulders were unmistakable—I'd seen him practically every day for three years by then. He saw me too, but didn't give any sign. I thought of turning back, I didn't want to see anyone. But I was traveling on inertia and I walked right up to him.

For a minute he just looked at me. Then he pulled my coat collar up around my ears. It was cold and the wind was whipping my hair around. He smoothed it back out of my eyes and held it back with both hands. I tried not to look at him, but he wouldn't let me turn my head away. He just looked at me until I started to cry. I hadn't cried at all before, but I cried then. He pushed my face into his sweater and held it there, both of his arms wrapped around my neck. I tried to push away, but he tightened his grip so I could hardly breathe. I stopped crying from sheer fear. When I did, he let me go and turned away from me, his hands in the pockets of his jeans, and I regretted my moment of fear.

He walked with me all the way to the lighthouse without saying anything. But on the way back he talked. He talked about his years in the navy and about his parents' house on Indian Neck beach, and about the sailboat he had then. He didn't seem to expect any response, and he asked me only one question, one that I thought about quite a lot, being Irish. He asked me if I knew that Irish fishermen refuse to learn how to swim because they believe it only prolongs the agony of drowning.

I DECIDED TO SWIM. I went back to work, went back to school. I made dean's list for the first time, made myself indispensable in the credit office, I was so efficient, such a good worker. I always seemed to work the same night as Mark McCloud—he made up the schedules—and, friends now, we took coffee breaks together, supper breaks. When the weather turned we would get sandwiches from the deli and eat them on a bench in the park you could see from his office windows.

He gave me two weeks off to study for final exams. I didn't expect to be paid for them, but my paycheck was not only the same, it was doubled. There was a note inside from the store manager wishing me good luck. I knew Mark had arranged that; the store manager didn't even know my name. When I went into his office to thank him, he asked me to have lunch. We went to the Clifford Hotel. I'd always paid for my own meals before, but he said this was a present. The bonus was a graduation present from the store, lunch would be his own present. He asked me all the usual questions: What are your plans now? What will you do? Where will you go? But they made me miserable. I didn't know what to do. I didn't have any plans. I hadn't thought any farther ahead than the summer. Michelle and I were going to Europe for a couple of months and I half expected that to somehow solve everything. I asked him if I could still have a job at Robertson's when I got back, if I could stay there until I decided what to do. He said yes, sure, of course, as long as I needed, as long as I wanted, forever.

We left the day after graduation and went to Portugal, then Spain, then Italy, spending longer than we'd planned in each place. We hadn't planned to go to Zurich at all, even though I still had the piece of paper in my wallet. In fact, I'd promised myself I wouldn't. I'd promised Michelle too, but I suddenly decided to go one night in July when we were sitting in the train station in Rome waiting for a train to Brindisi, so we could go to Greece. We had Eurail passes. We could go anywhere. I sat there looking at this train marked ZURICH until I couldn't stand it anymore.

We got into Zurich late at night. I didn't know any German at all, and after breakfast I asked the woman who ran the pension to place the call for me. Alfred did not seem at all surprised to hear from me, in fact he said a very strange thing. When I said, "Alfred, this is Margaret," he said, "Oh, that's what I was dreaming about." I told him where I was and he told me which tram to take to Paradeplatz. So I got on the tram, but I didn't know whether Paradeplatz was a street or a plaza or a building. I didn't know where to get off, or how to ask. I was looking out the window and saw Alfred standing on a corner. I looked straight into his eyes, entirely by accident. And this is how I choose to remember him: suddenly galvanized, running alongside the tram, shouting and waving, frantic.

We had lunch at a sidewalk cafe on the Limmat River. The last time we'd met I'd said nothing at all; this time I did most of the talking. I told him all about our time in Lisbon and at Estoril and Madrid and Florence and Rome. He talked a little about his job for a computer firm and showed me a picture of his daughter. I examined it politely, but she was nothing to me. He was very quiet. I thought he would go back to work after lunch, but he made a phone call instead. We went to the zoo and to the ceme-

tery. I wanted to see where Joyce was buried, I wanted to see the
lions whose roar Joyce had wanted to hear eternally. Alfred said
he didn't know that James Joyce was buried in Zurich, which
surprised me more than anything else he'd ever said or done.

He made another telephone call later and we got his car out
of a downtown garage and drove up into the mountains and had
dinner. He kept making phone calls. He kept fiddling with his
wedding ring, taking it off, tossing it in his hand, as if he were
trying to gauge its weight. We stayed out very late and said
good-bye on the sidewalk in front of the pension. I looked up
once and saw Michelle in her nightgown looking down from
our window on the second floor. But the next time I looked she
was gone. The last time Alfred kissed me I felt a drop of mois-
ture on his cheek, and I knew that this was what I had come for.
I had traveled a long way just to be the one to leave.

WHEN WE GOT BACK we both worked at Robertson's full time.
Michelle didn't have to be back at school until mid-September.
Mark was excited about a job he had found for me in Adver-
tising, where they needed a copy writer. I told him I would think
about it, and I was still thinking about it two weeks later when
they hired someone else. He was disappointed and a little angry.
He avoided me for days.

Then one night I was making my way back in the dark from
the employees' cafeteria. The store was closed. It was open only
one night a week now, but the suburban stores were open every
night and there had to be a skeleton staff on duty to authorize
charges. The rest of the store was in darkness and the cafeteria
was closed. But we had all learned how to make coffee or tea
and figured out where Bea stashed the day's leftovers. I had just
switched off the lights and was feeling my way down the narrow
corridor in the stock room that led from the back of the credit

department to the cafeteria, when I heard someone moving towards me in the dark and the top of my head went cold.

"Margaret?" he said. In the dark his voice sounded closer than it was and I waited for what seemed like a long time. I could feel him coming closer and closer, feeling his way along the wall. One of his hands brushed my face, lightly, the way a blind person does, seeking information, then rested there. His other hand moved up to my other cheek. I was mesmerized by the slowness of his movements, by the excruciating gentleness of his hands. Then the door to the credit department opened and slammed, Michelle's clogs clomped towards us in the dark. Mark went one way and I the other, still feeling his hand on my face, wanting to feel it again.

"What's going on?" Michelle said, on the way home that night. "He followed you out there. I watched him."

That was the last night Michelle and I worked together. We worked together during the day, but Mark never scheduled us for the same night again. There was an unspoken but not very subtle warfare going on. Michelle would switch with someone, then he would make a complicated contravening switch. I was being struggled over by two people I admired tremendously, a completely new and not at all unpleasant experience.

There were no more close encounters in the dark. There were opportunities which he did not take, not only, I think now, because he believed that indeed there would be time, but because there was another warfare going on, inside himself. Still, our relationship had openly shifted to a different plane. He started helping me lock up the files at the end of the night, something I'd done alone for four years. He'd slide out the heavy metal covers and take the keys from me, and stoop to lock the bottom files. The rest of the night staff stood by the elevators waiting, watching. Then we'd all get into the freight elevator and he would pilot us down the five floors to the street level, shut off the elevator, lock it, turn off the lights, unlock the employees' door to let us out into the alley, and lock it again after us. He'd walk me to my car and stand there with me, talking, until everyone else had driven away or their rides had come and gone.

He would do all these obvious things, but he didn't touch me again, until one night, as I was getting into my car, he asked if I wanted to take a walk on the beach. It was a hot, muggy night. I slid over and let him drive. We had trouble finding a place to park on the beach road, passing endless cars with shadows wrestling in the dark. Not only lovers but families would come out on hot nights, the kids in their pajamas, the windows rolled down for the breeze off the water. Finally, he switched off the engine. He pushed the seat back as far as it would go and slid down until his head rested on the top of the seat back. He closed his eyes briefly. Most of his face was in shadow. I sat with my back against the passenger door, looking at him, looking at the line of his throat and chin whitened by the fluorescent streetlight. I knew that I had only to reach out and trace that line with a fingertip, and my future would decide itself.

Then he opened his eyes and turned his head. He said, "This isn't what I want. I don't want to have an affair with you." I shook my head, no, I didn't want that either. But we moved into each other's arms anyway. There is nothing else quite like that, to be held, caressed, kissed by a man who wants you that much, who has wanted you that long.

When I got home, Michelle and my mother were sitting on the front porch. My mother looked at her watch, and Michelle gave me a look that said she knew exactly where I'd been and with whom. But neither of them said anything about it. Michelle said she had come over to talk me into driving down to Washington with her the next day. The next day was a Friday and she was going down to look for a place to live for her senior year.

All the way down there she talked about Washington, how glad she was to be getting back, about her friends, the things they did, the places they went. I knew what was coming. She wanted me to move there too. "Margaret, you have *got* to get out of there. Everyone is talking about you. I just hope my parents don't find out."

That night in Clyde's she ran into two friends from school who were in town for the same reason and hadn't had any luck with apartments. They all decided to go to a realtor together and look for a house to share. The very first house the realtor took us to the next day was a white brick with a red door, half a block down from the French Market in Georgetown. They all wanted it, they loved it, but the rent was too high for three. They needed a fourth, and they needed someone who was twenty-one to sign the lease. There was no time to look around for another person, this house wouldn't last a minute.

"Look," Michelle pleaded. "If you sign the lease, then you'll have to come. If you come, you'll have to find a job. It will all work out. Just throw your hat over the fence, why don't you?"

At first I said no. Then I just picked up the pen and signed. Immediately I felt relieved, saved.

My father was unhappy. He was back on his feet again, but he wanted me to stay home forever. My mother was deteriorating, but she wanted me to leave. "It's time," she said. "Go."

When I tried to give Mark two weeks' notice, he wouldn't listen. He said, "Agnes McPhee is leaving next month. You can have her job. I'll start you at two thousand over her salary. Three weeks vacation, ten days sick leave, five paid holidays." This was all he could say. The collection man was stationed at his desk right outside the open door.

"I signed a lease," I said. "I have to go."

"Cancel it. You can cancel it. Nine thousand life insurance, Blue Cross–Blue Shield, fifty-dollar deductible."

"No," I said. "I'm going. I want to go."

He didn't say anything else. He swung his chair around and sat facing the windows. I looked at his back a minute, then left. I picked up a telephone that was ringing. Michelle gave me a long look and then went back to her filing. A while later Mark put on his suit coat and went out.

On my last day he called me into his office and asked me to sit down. He shut the door. I noticed a pale band of flesh where his wedding ring had been, and my stomach went queasy with fear. But all he said was, "Will you write to me?"

"How can I write to you? Alice opens your mail."

"Mark it personal. She doesn't open anything personal."

"She knows my handwriting. Everybody knows my hand-writing."

"Type. You can type."

"I don't have a typewriter. Besides, there's the postmark."

"When you get a job," he said, "there'll be a typewriter. I'll get a post office box. You can write to me there."

"Don't get a post office box," I said. "I'm not going to write."

He put his hands on the desk, palms up. "Margaret," he said. "Please."

I went out and emptied the drawer at the bottom of the files where I'd kept extra shoes, sweaters, and books for four years. I was too upset to finish the day. I said good-bye to Agnes, Alice, Lizzie, and Kate. They all hugged me and said they would miss me but that they were glad I was going, that there was no future there for a young person. I took their words at face value, even though Michelle had told me people had been talking. I must have thought they couldn't see or hear, those older married women, or I must have thought I was invisible. When I left, Mark was standing up, looking out his window. I felt as if I was leaving home, sneaking out the back door.

I never saw that place again, or for years even thought

about it very much. My life filled up quickly with other places and people. But I had this dream and have been thinking about it all. Robertson's is no longer even there. The downtown store was razed years ago. But in the dream I take the employees' elevator up to the sixth floor, I walk down the hall to the credit office, turn the corner, and everything is exactly as it was. The odd-shaped fluorescent lights, the sloping wooden floors, the two rows of metal files with their twenty black telephones. Alice and Kate and Agnes and Lizzie are sitting on chairs, filing, talking, their cardigan sleeves pushed up to their elbows. I can even hear the snap of Lizzie's chewing gum and smell the disinfectant Agnes scrubbed the telephones with all winter.

In the dream, I'm not eighteen or twenty-two. I'm forty-four. But Mark McCloud is the same thirty years old he was then. He's sitting at his desk, and I can see him so clearly, his face, his kind gray eyes, his hands. And I'm so glad to see him again, so happy, so deeply moved. But when he looks up, he does what my present thirty-year-old employer does when I enter his field of vision. He does not even see me.

SIX OR SEVEN MONTHS later he sent me a poem. There was no letter, just a very long poem full of salt air, sea breezes, stolen kisses in a car, everything. But I knew too much about poetry to be moved. What gave me a pause, though, was thinking about him looking up my address in the files and seeing the charges I'd made at one of the suburban stores when I was home for Thanksgiving and had not come by to say hello.

I did see him again, three years later. Michelle had married George and I had my own apartment off Scott Circle. I didn't know he was coming. It was a complete surprise. I'd just driven back from Baltimore where I went after work every day to visit my mother, who was dying in Johns Hopkins, where my oldest sister, a doctor, had moved her after our father died. It was late and I was very tired, and very sad. When I let myself into the lobby, he stood up. He'd been sitting there for hours reading a *Washington Post*. He said he was in town for a conference at the Statler Hilton.

We went up to my apartment and I poured us some Scotch. I knew Tom would be along any minute. When I told him I was engaged he raised his glass to me. I saw he was wearing his wedding ring again. He told me that Jenny Hill had married and divorced the store detective and moved on to New York. I told him about Michelle's wedding, but he didn't really want to hear about Michelle. He told me that Kate Coyle had died. He told me I was lucky I hadn't taken Agnes's job, that Authorizing had been phased out entirely, all that work was now done by computers. Then he showed me the latest photographs of his children. I examined them carefully.

When Tom came they talked mostly to each other. They talked about baseball, which surprised me, because I didn't know that either of them was particularly interested in baseball. When Mark stood up to leave, Tom said we would drive him, that he shouldn't be out walking at that time of night. I sat in the middle, and when he was getting out of the car Mark reached across me to shake Tom's hand. "Take care," he said. "Take care of her." As he pushed through the revolving doors of the hotel, Tom said, "Who is that guy, anyway?"

There was just one other time. I didn't see him, but we talked on the telephone. It was another three years later. We had just come back from a year in England. I wondered how he got our telephone number. It didn't seem possible he would have remembered Tom's last name, from just hearing it once. And I didn't have a charge account at Robertson's anymore. Both of my parents were dead and I never went to Rhode Island. But credit people have access to all kinds of information.

He knew all about England. He had called the year before, when he first moved to Washington, and the people who were subletting our house had told him where we were, and when we would be back. He asked me how I was. I said, "Pregnant. Very pregnant."

He said that they'd had another baby, too, that she was nearly three years old now, that her name was Margaret, but they called her Megatron. I said that I liked that a lot, Megatron. I said that I couldn't believe he was living in Washington now. I asked what he was doing there. He said that he was the credit manager at Izak's.

"Oh," I said. "Izak's. We have a charge account there."

"I know."

He asked me to come by his office next time I was downtown. We could have lunch, and talk. I said I would. But I didn't. First I was pregnant, and I was going to graduate school part time. Then Sara was born and I was busy coping with a new baby, plus graduate school. Soon Tom got a job in Boston and we moved. We never changed our address at Izak's. We just didn't go there anymore.

Taking Off

They've just turned onto Highway 12, the last leg of the drive to the dunes, when Elaine sees the ominous cloud formation. A massive V of black-edged silver pillows zeroes into the flat red disc of sun that hangs over the horizon like a Japanese flag. The sky has been hidden by the canopy of trees along the road they took out of town. Duncan sees it at the same time.

"Must be the heat," he says. The temperature posted outside the bank back in town read 96 degrees at 6:30.

"What? What must be the heat?" Eric and Lisa lean over the seat backs to see. Eric says he hopes it isn't going to rain, on top of everything else, and slumps back into his corner. He's been waiting all day to go swimming, but his parents spent the entire afternoon in their room with the door shut. Every time he knocked to ask when they were going to leave, his father would say "soon," without opening the door.

"I think it's beautiful," Lisa says. "It looks like an angel turned upside down. The silver clouds are the gown. The sun is the head *and* the halo."

"It looks like dirty soapsuds going down the drain," Duncan says. "It looks like the whole damn sky is going down the drain."

Elaine looks at him. His lips are pale, the only color in his face the dark smudges under his eyes. She wants to tell him to take a good look in the mirror. She wants him to see how much trying to recover his lost youth, or whatever he's been trying to do, has aged him.

"Can I be an angel for Halloween?" Lisa has just turned seven. When nobody answers, she repeats. "Can I?"

"Ask your father," Elaine says, and out of the corner of her eye she sees Duncan's knuckles go white on the steering wheel.

A MONTH AGO SHE called her sister in Philadelphia, but knew as soon as she heard her voice that Kay had nothing to offer her. Kay had never married. She had no idea how thoroughly you can forget how to live alone. "Do you love him? Are you still in love with him? Is that it?" she'd asked hesitantly, after a long silence, and when Elaine said nothing, she reasoned with her. "I don't understand why you would want to keep him if he wants to go. I mean, what's the point?" The thing to do, Kay told her, was to take care of herself, keep her spirits up. "Get out more, see people."

But there wasn't anyone, not really. As Duncan moved up and down the precarious academic ladder and around the country Elaine had left her own friends farther and farther behind. She wasn't even working now. This last move two years ago had brought them to a small college town where anyone who didn't work for the university, or for the manufacturer of RVs, was unemployed. It was only a stopping place, Duncan had assured her. By the end of this three-year appointment he would have another book out and could move to a better place. He would get her to a city again, where she could get another job, make more friends of her own. Now she felt as if she were being put off a train in the middle of the night, in the middle of nowhere.

She had thought it might pass, that Duncan might get over

whatever it was, that as long as it remained unspoken between them it didn't really exist. So she didn't ask questions, didn't mention the phone calls and the sudden departures. Even when Duncan started staying up most of the night, lying on the floor in the living room, smoking cigarettes again and listening to music he hadn't played in years, she had said nothing. Then, recently, when she saw that he was looking for opportunities to tell her, she tried to circumvent them, leaving the room when he came in, getting up when he sat down.

He finally cornered her this afternoon while she was lying down instead of changing into her bathing suit. He walked into the bedroom and shut the door behind him. She didn't look at him. She continued to focus on the place near the ceiling where two seams of wallpaper, steamed off by the heat, were beginning to curl away from each other.

"Do you know what you want, Duncan?" she asked, after he told her.

"I don't want anything," he said, misunderstanding. "Just my books and my typewriter. I'll leave the computer. I want to keep the house as it is, for the kids."

He was sitting on the sofa across from the foot of the bed. She sat up and looked at him, willing him to realize that he'd misunderstood, that he'd skipped too many steps. But he smiled at her, relieved she was taking it so well, and all she said was, "Get your feet off my sofa."

THE SUN IS ABOUT to set by the time they spread their blanket on the beach. The sky over Chicago, across Lake Michigan, is a solid mass of black clouds now. But overhead it's still clear and there's no wind to blow the storm in their direction. There will be at least another hour of light. Elaine kicks off her shoes and walks off down the beach.

"Wait," Duncan says. "I'll come with you."

He calls to the children, who are already in the water. He tells Eric to keep an eye on Lisa, but Eric ignores him. He calls to Elaine to wait, but she keeps walking and he has to run after her, awkwardly, irritated by the smirks of the three teenage boys in sawed-off T-shirts who are moving towards him, spanning the narrow stretch of beach between the water and the dunes. They broke ranks to let Elaine pass, and glanced after her in a way he might once have resented but which now gives him a measure of comfort. But Duncan they force to sidestep into the water as they saunter past, flaunting their rude bodies and good health. The tallest yelps at him over his shoulder, "Go for it," and Duncan is as thrown off balance as if he'd been shoved.

Go for it.

Less than a month ago, he and Elizabeth walked a rural Michigan road, talking, for the last time, it seemed, about the impossibility of their situation. Their children knew each other; Eric was in the same class at school as Elizabeth's daughter and had even taken her to their sixth-grade dance. They would never forgive such public humiliation. Duncan was Elizabeth's advisor, the only one in her field. After three years of graduate work she would have to find something else to do. The university where both Duncan and Elizabeth's husband taught was zealously Catholic. When Elizabeth confided in a close friend, a lawyer, asking him about possible professional consequences, he had clucked sympathetically and jerked a thumb in the general direction of the campus. "Those nice people over there, sweetheart, will chew you up and spit you out in little pieces." They'd been talking about all this, yet again, when a yellow school bus lumbered past them, raising clouds of dust, and a small boy leaned out of a rear window and delivered what had seemed then a message of encouragement from the universe, a boisterous and cheerful, "Go for it!"

Since then Duncan had carried on imaginary conversations with Elaine, in which she listened with interest to all he had to say, in which she eventually understood his decision. But when he shut the bedroom door behind him this afternoon, he saw in the adjustment of her shoulders just how much energy she had spent in avoiding this conversation, how she held her whole body in opposition to him. And he'd been able to explain nothing. When he tried, Elaine put out her hand. "Spare me," she said. "Please, spare me the details."

He tried to tell her instead that he had no intention of abandoning his family, that he would come often, several times a week, to be with the children, to do what needed to be done around the house: trim the hedges, cut the grass, take down the awnings, shovel the snow. Even as he spoke he saw how mistaken he was.

"You'll have access to the children, of course," Elaine said. "But don't come around here for anything else. I can take care of myself." She was sitting up then, her long legs folded under her, and she raised her arms, pressed the heels of her hands against her temples in a gesture he had never seen before, one that made his scalp go cold. She looked as if she might scream, but her voice was measured, in control. "Once you leave, Duncan, that's it. You don't come back."

Immediately, he saw himself alone. Elizabeth's husband wouldn't let her go without a fight. He would fight and he would win. She would change her mind, and Duncan, having burned his bridges, would move his books and his typewriter into the first of the series of small apartments in which he would live alone for the rest of his life. On visitation days, he would arrive at the door of the house that had once been his, lingering awkwardly, waiting for the children. One day he would pull up in front of the house and find a man in the yard, trimming the hedges. The man would call to the children that their father was there. He would remind Eric he still had his geometry to do. He would send Lisa back for a sweater. He would go into the house and shut the door.

DUNCAN CALLS TO ELAINE again, surprised by the note of panic he hears in his voice. But she keeps walking, and he picks up a flat, smooth stone and lets it fly along the shoreline. It skims the water seven, eight, nine times, before vanishing. Elaine stops and turns around, waits for him to catch up. But when he does, he has nothing to say. Finally, she picks up a stone and throws it out over the water, where it sinks.

"I never could do that," she says.

"It's easy. I'll show you."

He looks around for one the right shape. He shows her what it should look like: flat, smooth, large but not too heavy. He shows her how to hold it in the curve of her forefinger and thumb. She starts to throw it, but he catches her arm. "No. Not like that. You've got to get a good backswing and then straighten your arm as you let it go."

His voice snags on the words, and he wonders what they're doing here now anyway. They had planned to take a family trip to the dunes today and they had gone, even though they'd suddenly stopped being a family. It reminds him of a photograph he once saw of executions during the Boxer rebellion in China; how the dead men's bodies would continue to run a few steps after their heads had been lopped off. He stands behind Elaine and stretches his arm along hers, guiding her hand back, and swings it forward. The stone flies straight up into the air, hits the water, and sinks. "Never mind," she says, and starts walking again.

He falls into step beside her and reaches out a hand to straighten the twisted strap of her bathing suit. She neatly deflects his hand and straightens the strap herself. They pick their way through a concentration of dead fish whose open-mouthed, rigid bodies litter the shoreline. Elaine wonders if the children should be swimming in water that kills so many fish, but Duncan tells her that it's not the pollution, it's the heat. "The water temperature is too high, the oxygen level drops. They suffocate."

He picks up a fish and dangles it between them. Perch. The fish stares at each of them with a sightless eye, mouth fixed open in silent astonishment. Duncan peers in at the delicate cage of bones and then pitches the fish into the lake. Elaine drops to her knees and clears a wide space, holding her breath, picking up fish by the tips of their tails and casting them away. "Jesus," she says, when she sees that the depressions they leave in the sand are alive with tiny white worms, wriggling in distress, rooting for their vanished hosts. Duncan picks up a stick and smooths the sand over them.

Elaine stretches out on her back and Duncan sits down next to her. He scans the sky. "The clouds are moving in," he says. "Storm coming." But Elaine closes her eyes. Her voice is even, without rancor, as if merely asking a question.

"Why did you have to leave me here, Duncan? Why didn't you leave when I had a job? When I had friends? Why did you wait until now?" Duncan looks at her in amazement. Can't she see that this has nothing to do with her?

"The worst part was the silence," she says. "All those months without talking. April, May, June, July, August. It's a long time to just wait." Again Duncan regards her in surprised silence.

It was a year and a half ago that he met Elizabeth, when she enrolled in his graduate seminar. A thirty-five-year-old wife and mother, she kept silent among all the younger students who were so confident, so sure of themselves, although Duncan soon realized she was smarter than all the rest of them put together. She took a second course with him last summer, and a third in the fall. By then he was working longer and longer hours at preparing his lectures. If he came into class and she wasn't there he felt betrayed, all his preparation for nothing. He looked forward to reading her papers as eagerly as if they were love letters. During Christmas break, a time he had always looked forward to before, he did nothing but count the days until the next semester could begin.

"It was on Memorial Day that I knew for sure," Elaine says. She waits a minute before going on, and then lays her words down one at a time, like carefully placed stones, as if, not knowing where they would lead, she might have to find her way back across them.

"You had a phone call and I went upstairs to get you. You'd said you had a lot of work to do, but you were asleep, lying across the bed. When I opened the door you rolled over onto your stomach, still asleep. Your change had fallen out of your pockets, and your keys. There was another key I didn't recognize. It was attached to a piece of wood in the shape of a pine tree. I picked it up and looked at it. It had the name of that lake in Michigan stamped on it. And the address. And the cabin number. I put it back. I closed the door, and I went downstairs again."

"Elaine." Duncan puts out a hand to touch her, but thinks better of it.

"I knew then that I'd known all along. All those weekends and holidays, Sundays, that you couldn't stand being home. You'd sleep through them. Still, it was like going to wake up your husband and finding a total stranger lying on your bed. I told whoever it was on the phone—I couldn't believe he was still there—I said, 'Duncan isn't here. I have no idea when he'll be back.' That was three months ago."

Duncan picks up the stick again and draws wide circles in the sand. He imagines the woman who owns the cottages telling Elaine that she'd guessed about those two right away. They'd both worn wedding rings, but she'd seen the look they gave each other when she asked for their address. When they finally put down Duncan's university address she figured she'd better mention that a man in the history department lived right down the road.

"Who else knows? Everybody?"

"No. No one." Duncan's response is immediate, self-right-eous, as if challenged on a point of honor. "Nobody knows." Elaine raises her eyebrows.

"Don't they?"

Duncan hears the woman telling the man in the history department all about them. How they never came on weekends or holidays, like other people did. How they'd arrive on a Monday or Wednesday morning, sometimes in one car and sometimes in another, and wouldn't emerge until noon. Then they'd stagger down to the platform swing halfway down the hill, carrying books and papers. After a while he'd go back up for coffee, or she'd bring down sandwiches. They'd picked all her best flowers: first the irises, then the day lilies, then the roses. They'd stick them in a jar on their kitchen table, the only trace they ever left behind. They never took a boat out, never set foot in the lake, never even glanced into the new game room her sons had built over the winter.

"What about the kids?" Elaine says. "Don't you think they know? Have you talked to them recently? Listened to them?" She tells him about a dream Lisa had a week ago.

"She was in the pantry watching two sticks of butter on a plate. The sticks of butter were you and me. In the dream she knew that if she looked away for even a second, they would start to melt."

Duncan thinks about his children, how they dwell in subterranean passages, picking up nonverbal signals, worrying. "It will be better for them when they know for sure," he says.

"Don't kid yourself." Elaine sits up abruptly and picks up the stick that he's abandoned, puncturing his wide circles with small, deep holes.

"You'll have to tell them yourself," she says after a while. "I'm not going to do it. And I'm not going to do it with you, no matter what they say you should do."

"I'll tell them tonight," Duncan says, and then after another silence, adds, "Do you think I should tell them together? Or talk to them one at a time?"

"Suit yourself," Elaine says, with a shrug. "It will be all the same to them, believe me."

"I'll steer clear of our friends," Duncan says, wanting to offer something, anything. "I won't tell anybody anything. You can say it's your decision, if you want."

"*Our* friends?" Elaine tosses the stick away. Their friends were Duncan's colleagues and their wives, or Duncan's colleagues and their husbands. She had gone to their houses for dinner and had invited them back in return. But they had exchanged nothing but food. They would avoid her now, she was certain.

"All those awful people. All those awful parties. All that goddamn food." Angry now, she looks at him. "Do you really think I'll stay here? Why should I stay here? I never wanted to come here in the first place."

"But, where will you go?" Duncan looks around, as if a strong wind has swept away every familiar landmark.

"I don't know. Back."

THE CONCESSION STAND IS closed and the beach in front of the bathhouse deserted. Lisa is standing near the blanket, wrapped in a towel, her thin legs clamped together, her eyes wide with scanning the horizon, looking for her parents.

"There's lightning," she calls, in her high, thin voice. "Eric's going to get electrocuted. I told him to get out. But he won't."

As if on cue, three rods of lightning jab silently in the vicinity of Chicago. In the past hour the wind has risen and rolled the black clouds overhead, lifting the water into angry little white lips.

"Tell him to get out," Elaine says.

Last summer they were here when a sudden late-afternoon storm blew up from the opposite direction. A ranger with a bull-horn had pulled up in a jeep and ordered everyone out of the water. When Duncan asked him if there was any real danger the man had looked at him for a moment with contempt. Then he'd told them that in the water you could be electrocuted by lightning five miles off. "Fried" was the word he'd used. He told them about three men who'd been fishing, who'd been electro-cuted in a wooden boat that had taken on just three inches of water. They'd been dead for two days when their boat drifted into Benton Harbor one morning just before dawn.

"There's no real danger," Duncan says. "The lightning is at least ten miles away. Otherwise, we'd hear the thunder."

"Get out this instant, Eric!" Elaine yells. But Eric rolls over on his back and ignores her. Behind her, she hears Duncan's voice, indulgent, full of understanding for all human failing. "Listen to your mother, Eric." But, one disaster having over-taken them, she imagines another. She can actually see the electric current moving through the water toward the boy, like a shark. She wades in and grabs his arm, roughly drags him out.

"Lemme alone." He shakes her off and treads his way out of the water.

Duncan tosses Eric a towel, man to man, and lights a ciga-rette. Tired of waiting, afraid of the storm that is obviously almost upon them, Lisa says she's going to the car and starts laboring her barefooted way through the deep sand to the parking lot behind the bathhouse. Not anxious to leave, to go home, Duncan inhales deeply, examining the sky. Then he throws his cigarette away and watches the wind take it rapidly sideways down the beach and out of sight.

"I guess we'd better go," he says. "It's moving more quickly than I thought."

But they remain standing, even Eric, and both Elaine and Duncan know now that he already knows. Only Lisa wants to go home. She turns her back on them once more and heads purposefully towards the parking lot. Elaine watches her for a minute, then bends over the blanket picking up thongs, shorts, towels, shaking the sand from each object.

All at once, she feels the temperature drop. It's like a cold, wet towel slapped across her back. Even before she straightens, she hears Duncan. "Shit! Here it comes." She hears the wind roaring at her like a freight train. She sees Duncan's hands snatch futilely at the corner of their blanket. She starts to run. In the distance, she can see Lisa, still wrapped in the towel, struggling against the wind, her small legs stiff as twigs, her astonished gaze fixed on the agile trees that are stretching themselves flat across the tops of the dunes.

Just as she reaches Lisa and takes hold of her hand, acres of sand are lifted into the air and all is eclipsed by a dense, white darkness. The whirling sand whips their faces, their bare arms and legs, stinging like a swarm of hornets. Elaine tries to push Lisa to the ground, to shield her. Lisa, not understanding, sends up a peal of screams. Then Duncan, behind them, pushes at Elaine, the flat of his hand a power between her shoulder blades.

"Move," he yells, as if from a great distance. "Keep moving!"

But it is almost impossible to move. Heads bent against the swirling sand, they trudge blindly, drunkenly, the wind wrapping around their legs like voluminous wet skirts. Discussion is out of the question, but Elaine knows they are wrong to resist. She has read, on the posters tacked to the walls of all public buildings in this part of the world, what they should do in the event of a tornado. They should lie flat, face-down in a ditch with their arms over their heads. But there are no ditches here, and she imagines them all stretched out flat across the sand, holding hands, lifted like a string of paper dolls, taking off, ripped apart in the air.

Paper cups and empty soda cans bombard their legs. A wire trash basket, plucked from its pole, sails in front of them like a dark shadow, displacing a great suck of air. Then Lisa, ahead of Elaine by a step, runs into the low edge of cement wall that defines the bathhouse area and is knocked on her back by the impact. Duncan picks her up and carries her. Elaine grabs Eric and pushes him in front of her in the direction of the building. They feel their way along the cinder block wall until their hands touch the wood of a door. Elaine pushes against it. Then Duncan sets Lisa down and pulls at the handle, prying the door open against the wind. He pushes them all inside.

As her fear subsides in the relative silence and her lungs fill again, Elaine is aware of the cold damp tile underfoot, and the smell of stale urine. "Get up." She nudges Eric with a foot. "Don't sit on the floor." But this time she doesn't care when he ignores her. Duncan is holding Lisa, who has sand in her torn knees, in her eyes. "Mommy!"

But Elaine turns a deaf ear. She rests her forehead against the moist tile wall. She counts their losses: towels, shorts, shirts, shoes, wallets, car keys, house keys. For a moment she imagines that the wind that swept all those things away has taken with it everything and everyone else in the world. They alone are safe. They will walk out of here into a world swept clean.

But she knows that tomorrow they will come with the spare keys to get the car. They will notify the Motor Vehicles about their lost licenses. They'll call the bank and the credit card companies. One by one, they will replace all of the things they have lost, except what they lost without even noticing. Duncan won't be able to tell the kids tonight. But tomorrow no disaster will save them.

"We're safe now," Duncan is telling Lisa. "It's not a tornado, just a lot of wind and sand. It'll blow over. You'll see. Then the ranger will come for us. He'll see our car. He'll take us home. Somebody will take us home." He already feels guilty, as if the storm was his fault. He already knows that everything that goes wrong for the rest of their lives will somehow be his fault. He touches Lisa's wet hair with his cold lips. He amends his promise.

"We're safe for now."

Holly's Landing

My stepfather met my mother in the summer of 1936 on the porch of the big white house in Marblehead built by her great-grandfather half a century before, and brought us back to northern California to the timber house he had built for his first wife above the mouth of the Russian River. I see the two events as one, although I know there must have been introductions, conversations, arrangements. I see my stepfather in a three-piece black suit walking up the steps as my mother, dressed in summer white, rises to take his hand. Then I see the three of us drifting down the steps of that house and up those of the other three thousand miles away.

My stepfather's house was longer and broader than ours, and was shingled in dark brown wood that had weathered to black. But the shape and the slopes and the angles were the same, and both houses were wrapped around three sides by wide, screened porches. Perhaps because of all the things that happened there, beginning with my mother's death in giving birth to stillborn twins, my stepfather's house sometimes seems to me to be a long shadow cast by the other.

But I was not unhappy there. For a while I missed my mother. But only for a while. And as I had been a posthumous child, I missed my father not at all. It was my stepfather I mourned years later, my stepfather and his Japanese housekeeper Nisi. By the time I was shipped back to Marblehead I had lived with them for a much longer time than I had lived with my mother. And if I had spoken at all, I would have told them that I was content.

In the Marblehead house we had lived with my mother's older sister, my uncle, and their six children. I had shared a bedroom with three cousins and a bed with one. But in my stepfather's house I had to myself a wide front bedroom with two sets of casement windows that opened out to the giant holly tree that grew in front of the house and inspired its festive name.

It was the tree that won my wavering allegiance when we first arrived at Holly's Landing. It stretched high above the roof of the house and was as tapered at the top as a Christmas tree. The branches that grew down to the ground on the back side gradually tapered upwards in front to expose a good five feet of smooth white bark marred by twin boles of greenish gray. The shiny dark leaves had pale undersides that lifted and caught the light in a breeze so that the whole tree shimmered like a silver lamé gown worn by a voluminous and slightly blowzy woman, arrested in the act of indelicately raising her skirts to reveal a pair of soiled knees.

Of her sex I am certain, because every spring she bore large clusters of pink buds. I always waited for those pink buds to open into pink flowers, but they never did. The flowers, year after year, were wax white with only the merest hint of purple outline. Her fruit, already ripening when we arrived that fall, held hard brown seeds that my stepfather told me were fertilized indiscriminately by the three or four dwarf males lurking nearby.

My stepfather also told me that the holly tree possessed many secret cures and weapons, so many that it was six years before I learned them all, learned, for example, that the waxy leaves contain highly flammable oils, that they ignite and roar like blowtorches in a fire. My stepfather showed me only one of her secrets.

I had never seen hummingbirds before and was enchanted by those that hovered over the back porch flower box on my first morning at the Landing. Through the kitchen window they looked like so many abbreviated fingers drumming accelerated time in the air. I wanted to get a closer look, but they vanished as soon as I stepped onto the porch. That afternoon my step-father took a pocketknife from his coat and cut a swath of bark from one of the small holly trees. He scraped the sticky flesh from the bark into a bowl and mashed it with a fork, then spread it along the rim of the flower box.

Next morning, all but one of the birds escaped. Its toes were stuck in the glue and it could do nothing but beat its blurred wings like a heart gone wild. It fluttered terrifyingly between my thumb and forefinger when I tried to pry it loose. Within a few hours it had beaten itself to death. My stepfather was off in his Studebaker, making the rounds of his patients, so it was Nisi who severed the bird from its feet and freed it for burial, muttering to herself all the while about the hardheartedness of doctors.

Nisi and my stepfather seemed always to be angry with each other, although she was devoted to my mother, and throughout my first year there I was afraid that she wouldn't stay or that he would send her away. But after my mother died I knew she would never leave. I was four when I went to live in California, and five when my mother died. There was a lot of talk at the time of sending me back to Massachusetts, but I saw no reason why I should go. After each letter from my aunt arrived I would hear Nisi and my stepfather arguing. Whenever they men-tioned Marblehead in my hearing I would disappear, sometimes for a whole day. Eventually Nisi, who wanted me to stay, would find me. She would carry me from my hiding place and present me to my stepfather. They would regard each other in silence for some time, then my stepfather would take me on his lap.

After the letters stopped, my aunt began sending me two

dolls for Christmas and birthdays instead of the single dolls I'd been given before. They were always the same dolls. My aunt made them herself to sell to neighbors, friends, and to any of my uncle's patients who waited captive in her parlor. My uncle and my stepfather had shared rooms at medical school, which is how he had come to visit us in Marblehead. Most likely, the day he found my mother on the porch her lap was full of material for the doll clothes she helped my aunt to sew, and she couldn't have risen to take his hand.

I didn't care for the dolls, for their silly painted faces and their fancy clothes. To please Nisi, I would finger their satin dresses or touch the miniver trim on their matching hats, but I never picked them up or held them. It was Nisi who carried them up to my room and placed them on shelves, and carried them down on Christmas Eve to air their dusty dresses before arranging them in pairs up the front stairway.

I was much more interested in drawing back the heavy russet curtain that concealed the space under the first curve of the stairway. This was where my stepfather kept the shortwave radio equipment he never used anymore. He had two sets, his old crystal set housed in a brown box with a brass clasp Nisi polished every Thursday, and the Sky Champion my mother had given him for their first and only Christmas. This set had all of the shortwave bands and the standard broadcast band. It had nine tubes that lit up and seven knobs on the front panel I would fiddle with for hours bringing in my favorite programs: *The Singing Lady*, *Tom Mix*, *Bobby Benson*, *Captain Tim's Stamp Program*, and *Amos and Andy*. Nisi loved the music of the big bands and she would turn up the volume and sing over it as she dusted down the banister. This always drove my stepfather out of his study and down the hill. Nisi said it was because he had no music in his soul, but he said it was because Nisi had no music in her voice.

It was the Sky Champion that brought us the news of the fall of France. It would also have brought us the news of the invasion of Poland, of Denmark, Norway, the Netherlands, Belgium, but it was the fall of France that I remember, because Nisi ran weeping to the bathroom and locked herself in for hours. I took comfort from the fact that my stepfather seemed, if not uninterested, at least unmoved. He barely lifted his eyes from the book he was reading when the bulletin interrupted *The Singing Lady*. When Nisi refused to answer my knocking at the door, he told me to let her be. He said she was probably upset because her brother would have to fight if America went to war.

But the next morning when I knelt beside her weeding the green-onion beds she said, "It's because he has no faith in life that he has no fear for it." At first I thought she meant Hitler, but as she went on muttering I realized that she was talking about my stepfather. Because I didn't speak, Nisi often pretended that I couldn't hear.

I knew even then she was wrong about my stepfather. He had nothing if not faith in human nature, faith as indiscriminately fertilized as the seeds of his holly tree. I think of him as a deeply religious man, but he would have objected to that. Only once did he take me into a church, and that was because a sudden winter rainstorm caught us on the edge of the neighboring village of Cobh without umbrellas or coats. He stood in the doorway looking out at the rain, while I amused myself collecting narrow pamphlets, taking one of each color, from the rack in the vestibule. He smiled when I prodded him with the stack of pamphlets and shook his head. "That's too much religion for anyone. It clogs the brain," he tapped his chest, "deadens the heart."

But the bedtime stories he told me were as likely to be taken from the Old Testament or Foxe's *Book of Martyrs* as from Aesop or Grimm. He knew the lives of all the saints as thoroughly and

intimately as he knew the case histories of his patients. "All that
is worth knowing," he told me, "can be learned from the lives of
courageous men and women."

When Nisi's younger brother Mitchi, after a long appren-
ticeship in San Francisco, set up as a shoemaker in Cobh and
asked him to suggest a name for his shop, my stepfather said
without hesitation, "Crispin. You should call it Crispin's." He
said no more, although Mitchi, not yet acquainted with my
stepfather's ways, waited in polite silence for some minutes.
That night, after Nisi had tucked me in and kissed me, my stepfather said, "It might as well be Crispin. You will have been
turning that name over and over in your head." And as if I had
agreed, he began his story about the patron of shoemakers.

"Actually, there were two of them, two brothers. Both were
martyrs who lived in the reign of Diocletian. *Regno, regnare.* To
rule, to reign. They traveled on foot from Rome to the north of
France where they settled at Soissons on the Aisne River. They
earned a living mending shoes. They were Christians, mind
you, in a pagan era, but they were, I like to think, unobtrusive
about their faith. I imagine them hanging a crudely fashioned
cross, no more than two sticks tied together with a leather
string, on the wall among their strips of hide. Only when they
were questioned about it would they give instruction. And then
dispassionately, good-humoredly, without perhaps missing a
stitch. At any rate they lived peacefully in their adopted village
on the river and made, they thought, no enemies.

"Then one day the famous soldier Maximian Herculius
stopped in Soissons on his way to or from some campaign or
other. It was the year after he'd been named Caesar and the year
before he was named emperor. He was still very anxious to suc-
ceed. I don't know how he came to hear of the brothers. He may
have ventured into their stall himself and caught sight of the
cross. More likely, their names were mentioned to him by an

equally ambitious gossip at the inn, perhaps by an apprentice shoemaker who hoped to set up his own shop in Soissons without competition. That's usually how these things happen. At any rate, the brothers were arrested. There was a trial at which they refused to defend themselves against the trumped-up charges. They were found guilty of subversion and, after severe torture, they were decapitated. Their heads were cut off. *De*, of separation. *Caput*, head. Shakespeare has given them immortality in the speech King Henry V makes to his troops on the eve of the battle of Agincourt.

> This story shall the good man tell his son,
> And Crispin Crispian shall ne'er go by,
> From this day to the ending of the world,
> But we in it shall be remembered—
> We few, we happy few, we band of brothers."

It was my stepfather's custom, unless he was called to a patient, to stay in my room until I had fallen asleep. He would switch off the lamp, push open the windows farthest from my bed, and stand there breathing in the rhythmic way he had taught me was the body's only defense against disease. But the night of the Crispin story he continued to talk as he stood with his hands in his pockets looking out at the holly tree.

"Immortality is not for everyone," he said. "It's reserved for those who stand firm against the winds of fortune and the vagaries of history. *Vagari*, to wander. History is the record of human progress. But it is full of vagabonds."

Although I think I learned as much from Nisi's muttering, it was my stepfather who undertook my education. He taught me what he knew, weaving stories from the lives of people he admired, poring over anatomy charts and naming every muscle, bone, and organ, always holding up words to reveal their long roots. He took me for long walks through the woods to the river and the landing where the sailboats he had had to sell long before I came to California had been moored. Or he took me down the long evergreen drive to the road that led into Cobh, naming everything along the way, trees, plants, flowers, birds, animals, buildings and the people in them.

"It's the ability to name, above all, that confers strength. That's why in Genesis we have God bringing all the animals to Adam so that he could name them and become their master. You only fear what you cannot name." I knew then why he had no fear of Hitler. He had named him vagabond. But I wondered why my stepfather never called me by my name, and why I had no name for him.

When we walked into Cobh he used to take me into the Belmont Bar and lift me onto a high stool covered with red leather. I liked nothing better than to sit there while my stepfather drank a small glass of whiskey, a large glass of beer, and traded news with Monty and the men who came to his tavern every afternoon. I liked the narrow glasses of ginger ale and the bowls of salted peanuts Monty pushed across the counter to me. I liked the look and the feel of the sawdust on the floor, the smell of whiskey and beer and cigarette smoke. I liked the sounds of the men's voices, the clink of bottle against glass, the knocking of the heavy metal pucks the men shuffled across the long table at the back of the room.

But Nisi objected to my being taken into a saloon, as she called it, and to reduce by one the number of things they argued about, my stepfather began depositing me in Mitchi's shop for an hour when we walked into town. I missed sliding the peanuts out of their skins, and the ginger ale, but I liked the smell of polish and leather, the hum of Mitchi's sewing machines, and the metallic taps of his hammer almost as much as the smells and sounds in the tavern.

Sometimes I poked among the rows of boots and shoes, pulling them out, looking behind them for two sticks tied together with a leather string. But this irritated Mitchi, and whenever I began moving around his shop he would dash across the street and come back with a new comic book. So I learned to content myself with climbing into one of the three outsize padded chairs set on a high platform, watching Mitchi's customers come and go, waiting for my stepfather's face, always a shade brighter after his visits with Monty, to appear at the window.

Our walks home ended at the holly tree. When I realized that it upset him to watch me embrace the tree, I began waiting until my stepfather had disappeared around the side of the house, where to avoid Nisi he would let himself in through the long windows of his study. Then I would wrap my arms around her and cool my forehead against her smooth white bark. As I grew older I tried to omit this ritual, but I had too thoroughly and for too long invested the tree with feeling and was nagged by guilt until I had greeted her in my usual way.

My stepfather loved the tree too, I knew. One day he laughed out loud in the Cobh library when he showed me a passage about the English holly in the big book of trees I wanted to take out. It said that the tallest tree lived in Port Deposit, Maryland, and was seventy-four feet high. Our tree, he told me, was ninety-two feet high and thirteen feet around.

"What do you think?" he asked me. "Should we write to them, or should we keep our secret?"

But our tree was no secret. There were occasional offers of high prices from a cabinetmaker in San Francisco who wanted the creamy wood for inlay. My stepfather said he was a bandit who would stain it black instead, and pass it off as ebony. He told me everything about the tree except what I wanted most to know. Would it live forever?

I had always thought that it would, until countries began to fall like trees all over Europe. After listening to the radio at night I would go to bed and, no matter what bedtime story my stepfather told me, I would fall into dreams that became night-mares of a giant lumberjack gone mad, hacking his way across the globe, moving closer and closer every night.

In the daylight it was possible to take comfort from measuring the great masses of land and water on the map that separated us from Hitler. But while we looked from our safe perch across the continent and out the front door of the Atlantic, war came to Holly's Landing through the back door.

It was Mitchi who brought us the news of the Japanese attack on Pearl Harbor. He was already in the kitchen with Nisi when I came down to breakfast one morning. I remember that I was far less shocked by the news than I was by the fact that brother and sister sat at the table while my stepfather stood, bending over Nisi, a steadying hand on each of her shoulders.

The next time Mitchi came it was to tell us that he'd just been to the bank where they had refused to cash his customers' checks and told him that he could no longer draw any money from his account, that bank credits of all Japanese had been frozen by federal order. He shook his head in disbelief.

"But I'm American. I was born here. Our parents were born here."

After that Mitchi came every day and had all of his meals with us. For a week or two he continued to open his shop every morning. But he told us that aside from the few customers who had come to pick up their shoes, the only people who came near his shop were the boys who pelted it with eggs. My stepfather persuaded him to give up his room over the Belmont. Nisi moved her bed up to my room and gave up her ground-floor room to her brother. Soon Mitchi didn't leave the house at all. He spent a good part of every day at the kitchen table, composing letters to President Roosevelt.

The radio became the center of our existence, the radio and the newspapers my stepfather brought home every day. They brought nothing but bad news. Japanese conquests in the Pacific, Japanese spies arrested. Every day my stepfather also brought home new rumors he had picked up in Monty's, rumors of periscopes sighted in Drake's Bay, a Japanese plot to blow up the Golden Gate Bridge, Japanese signaling to the enemy from Mount Tamalpais. I understood very little of all this. The only thing that was clear to me was that my stepfather and Nisi, at war for years, were now allies.

He never teased her anymore, and there were no arguments. Still, Nisi never smiled, and had developed a bad cold. Her nose and eyes were raw from stabbing at them with a handkerchief. Whenever my stepfather brewed pots of tea for her, it only made her cry. And it was only now that they were at peace that he talked of sending her away.

He tried to persuade both her and Mitchi to go east. He told them that my uncle in Marblehead would take them in and give them a home until it was safe to come back to California. But both brother and sister refused to leave. Mitchi was indignant when my stepfather spoke to him about it. Mitchi had changed too. Mitchi who had always held himself so tall, proud of his height and his handsome head, now looked guilty and ashamed.

I didn't go into Cobh again until a few days before Christmas when my stepfather took me to the drugstore to buy a blue box of talcum powder for Nisi and a fountain pen for Mitchi. No one spoke to us in the store, although my stepfather greeted several people by name. When he asked the unfamiliar woman behind the counter where her husband was, she laid his change on the glass top without a word and turned away.

As we crossed the street to look at Mitchi's shop I saw why he was so ashamed. Hundred of cracks radiated from a dozen small holes in the window. The glass door was covered with soap drawings of oriental faces, and a piece of cardboard hung from the doorknob by a string. I didn't see what it said because my stepfather folded it and put it in his pocket. Then he bent down and raised the flaps of a long box that sat on the threshold. Inside were four pairs of women's shoes, polished and new looking, their owners' names and the amounts still due printed on yellow tags in Mitchi's meticulous hand. He closed the flaps and stood up, his hands in his pockets.

"Take a good look," he said. "I want you to remember this."

The sidewalk was littered with rotting shells from the eggs that smeared the sign, Mike's Shoe Shop, that Mitchi had hung three years before after rejecting my stepfather's suggestion in favor of the more American name. I looked again at the drawings on the door and tried to rub one out with my sleeve, but it had been drawn with indelible hatred. I took my stepfather's hand and pulled him away. As we turned to go he kicked the box of women's shoes into the gutter.

We didn't go into the Belmont Bar. I never went there again. But I think it was that night that Monty and another man came to see my stepfather. Nisi disappeared into the kitchen and my stepfather opened the door for them. But he didn't ask them in. They stood in the doorway talking in low voices, while I took advantage of the chance to find something other than news on the radio. I was absorbed in moving the red station marker up and down the incandescent yellow band and paid no attention to the men. So I was startled to look up into Monty's flushed face, startled when my stepfather abruptly ordered me to bed.

I know that it was Christmas Eve that four men came dressed in overcoats and wearing hats, because Nisi was kneeling on the steps arranging the dolls in pairs and I was taping sprigs of holly around the mirror that hung in the front hall. And I know that they didn't knock, because I would have heard it. They seemed many more than four the way they came in all at once and swarmed through the house like so many

noiseless spiders. It was Nisi's screams that brought my stepfather from his study, and sent me running out the front door.

Some time later my stepfather pried my fingers from the
tree and carried me into the house. As he set me down in the
front hall I saw that the space under the curve of the stairway
was empty, except for the table that had held the radio and
shortwave equipment. The men had taken other things too: the
Winchester rifle that had hung behind my stepfather's desk, the
camera my mother had brought with her from Massachusetts,
the pair of outsize binoculars that were never used because they
didn't focus properly, the map of the world I had kept in my
room to trace in red ink the path of destruction to our door.

Nisi didn't get up on Christmas morning because her cold
was much worse. Mitchi and I carried trays up to my room and
ate our breakfast with her there. My stepfather was back from
his rounds before we were finished, his pockets bulging with
small objects wrapped in colored comics. Nisi said something in
Japanese. Mitchi took the breakfast trays down the back stairs
to the kitchen and came back with two large cartons. I rum-
maged under my bed for the talcum powder, the fountain pen,
and the white enamel shaving cup and brush Mitchi had helped
me to buy for my stepfather. I had made another present
for Mitchi to hang in his shop, but I decided not to give it to
him now.

There were not many presents to open, but we made the
ceremony last the morning by unwrapping them carefully, one
at a time, each of us by turn. From my stepfather were seven different colors of clay, each in its own wrapping. When I had laid
them out on my table like so many strips of bacon, Nisi called
me and patted the bed beside her. On her lap was a pile of small
packages she doled out to me one at a time. When they were all
opened there was a row of wooden dolls, each shaped like twin
egg cups fastened together and elaborately painted in bright

colors. Only the smallest doll was carved of a single piece of wood. Nisi waited until I had turned each doll over and over in my hand before showing me their secret. Then she opened the second smallest doll and concealed the smallest inside it. Each doll exactly fit inside the next until there was only one doll, heavily pregnant with the rest. I took them apart and lined them up, put them together again. Then Mitchi stood. He had saved his presents for last.

For my stepfather and Nisi he had made wine-colored slippers identical except for the beads he had sewn in swirls across the toes of Nisi's. For me there was a pair of soft leather shoes of holly-berry red with tapered wooden heels. I untied my oxfords, pulled off my socks, and slipped my bare feet into my first pair of grown-up shoes. Nisi and Mitchi clapped their hands in approval as I spun around the room, but when I came to a halt in front of my stepfather, he smiled sadly and looked away.

We spent the whole day in that room, presided over by our Christmas tree outside the windows. My stepfather read *A Christmas Carol* to us. He and Mitchi brought us a dinner of soup and apples and almonds. They played game after game of chess, while Nisi read the papers and dozed, and I fashioned dozens of hummingbirds in seven different colors. Whenever I take apart my days at Holly's Landing, line them up, turn them over, put them together again, that day is the one inside of which all the others slip exactly into place.

I HAD ALREADY OUTGROWN the red shoes before my stepfather put into words what he must have been thinking that morning. "You're not a child anymore. You can't go on living with a man who is no relation to you." If Nisi had been there, he would never have spoken to me that way. The harshness had crept into his voice with her going. And now I was going too. "You need things I can't give you. You need a home, a family. You need a woman's care."

What was left of Holly's Landing was up for sale. But even before it was sold my stepfather was going to Utah to join the medical staff at Topaz. Mitchi was already there. He'd been transferred a month before from the assembly camp in California he and Nisi had been sent to, the camp where Nisi, never fully recovered from her bronchitis, had died shortly after being inoculated against typhoid by one of the pharmacists who served as doctors at the camp.

There was no real reason for my stepfather to stay. The number of his patients had dwindled steadily until there were none left. Still, I think he felt he had to justify his decision to me, because my last night there, after he switched off the light in my room—the room that had been Nisi's, then Mitchi's, then mine after fire destroyed the front part of the house—he sat on the edge of my bed and put one of his hands over one of mine.

"Not very long ago," he said, "in New York, a great Frenchman spoke on behalf of Spain. He said that there is much suffering in the world and each of us must choose our own way of relieving it. But relieve it we must. I believe that. That is all I believe."

I would like to say that I sat up and put my arms around his neck, that I gave him some sign I understood. But I didn't understand. I withdrew my hand and rolled away from him.

There were no good-byes to say the next day. As we packed my suitcases into the car, I tried not even to look at the blackened stump of the holly tree, burned the night Japan captured Manila.

My stepfather said nothing all the way to Oakland where he turned me over to the three nursing students from San Francisco, bound for the Mediterranean, who had agreed to see me as far as New York where my uncle would meet the train. It was to them he talked on the station platform, while I counted the numbers of men in uniform.

But as the train pulled out of the station and I saw him walking away, so much older, his hands plunged deep into the pockets of the same black suit he had worn that day in Marblehead when my mother, so I still imagine, rose to take his hand, the words I had not said to him formed themselves.

"Father." I stood up on my seat and let down the window. "Father," I called again.

Too late, or perhaps my voice rang only in my own ears. If he heard me, he gave no sign.

Still in Mississippi

W hen she turned off the southbound highway she seemed to have been on since she left Chicago, and followed Taylor's white Corvette through a warren of back roads, she felt like Alice chasing the white rabbit down the rabbit hole, tunneling into the earth rather than riding on top of it. On either side of the sunken roads, which were not much wider than her secondhand Plymouth, great gnarled arms of tree roots muscled their way down through crumbling walls of earth. She had to look up to see where the trunks of the trees began. Moldy, lichened, twisted with Tarzan vines, they leaned precariously toward the road, their upper branches mingling, weaving a solid canopy of shade. It was so dark after the blinding sunlight on the highway and looked so cool she took off her sunglasses and let down her window. She turned her face full to the rush of air and was nearly flattened by the heat that swept over her like a steamroller. "Come in June," Taylor had said on the telephone. "Before it gets hot." .

She followed him through a pair of wooden gates marking the entrance to Glynwood, where Taylor's family had lived since the beginning of time. But then they seemed to move even more deeply into the woods, its character changing, the proportion of pine trees increasing dramatically: tall southern pines with clean, naked trunks and great tufts of long, pale needles. "We grow pencils and paper," he told her back in Chicago, when she'd asked him about cotton. "Tables and chairs. It's all timber."

She tried to remember, looking up through her windshield, what kind of tree it was that Taylor had said he and his sister used to shoot giant balls of mistletoe out of at Christmastime, and nearly rear-ended him as he braked for a sudden turn in front of a long, squat log-and-mortar house. In the clearing before the house, which was easily a hundred years old but not at all what she'd imagined, she counted half a dozen chickens pecking at dried cow dung, four dead or disabled vehicles, and a duck that must have had a turkey in its background somewhere, from the looks of the fleshy red growth on its forehead. "Jesus," she said. But Taylor didn't stop and she realized that this must be where Samson lived. She'd heard a lot about Samson.

It was another half mile through the woods before they got to Taylor's house. No wonder he'd said, "You won't find it," when she called him from the gas station on the highway to ask for directions. "There aren't any directions. I'll be right there." Now as the house finally swung into view around the last bend in the gouged and winding road, she remembered his description: a big, white two-story house that had seen better days and a lot more paint. Four white chimneys symmetrically sectioned the long black roof, and in a neat row at the back of the house where they parked were four small outbuildings Taylor had told her were the icehouse, smokehouse, summer kitchen and cook's house, all made of split logs worn smooth and gray, all used for storage now.

She knew it was the Chicago winter as much as his mother's illness that had driven Taylor south in March. It was last September when he moved in with Lisa and the children.

By February he was looking for spring, getting more and more depressed every day it delayed. "How long does this go on?" he'd asked her. "Doesn't it ever end?" He'd never seen such unreasonable weather. "The wind blows in your face; you turn around and walk the other way and it *still* blows in your face." By the time spring finally arrived he'd been gone a month already. He'd left the day after his sister called to tell him it was his turn to go home.

"*This* is reasonable weather?" Lisa called, as they got out of their cars. "It must be two hundred degrees."

"Never happened before, not this early. I swear." Taylor raised both hands.

They went in through the back door and, after pulling Lisa into the butler's pantry for a more passionate reunion than the one they'd had in front of the five old men sitting outside the gas station, Taylor led the way down a wide central hallway toward another door at the opposite end. Glancing briefly into dim, high-ceilinged rooms with yellowed, peeling wallpaper, carpets worn paper-thin, smoke-darkened portraits, and oddly placed pieces of furniture from a dozen different eras, she felt a weight descending on her from the sheer accumulation of years in one place. But when she stepped onto the gallery at the end of the hall she caught her breath, completely taken by surprise, although she remembered now that Taylor had also described to her what he'd called the park.

Shaded by a multitude of wide live-oak trees dangling long gray fingers of Spanish moss, it stretched from the steps a quarter of a mile to a small oval lake. Seeing it for the first time in the last of the light was like stepping into a painting, one long remembered and half forgotten, and as she looked and looked, three high riderless horses, manes and tails waving, thudded silently across the bottom of the frame. In the rose-tinged golden haze of early evening, they seemed ethereal, the ghosts of former horses. Then, suddenly breaking the spell, they plunged into the water, thrashing from side to side, shaking themselves furiously.

"Horseflies," said a deep, throaty voice behind her. "They drive us all mad. I told Taylor not to bring you here in horsefly season. But he said it would be too hot for you later."

THEY CARRIED THEIR SECOND round of drinks down the steps and walked through the grass, toward the lake. Twice, while she was looking up, Taylor took her arm and steered her around the conical nests of fire ants she nearly stepped on. Merritt, Taylor's mother, was pointing out how the Spanish moss that looked so romantic and benign was actually a vicious parasite strangling the live-oak trees to death.

"It's time to torch them again," she said, and Taylor explained how it was done.

"You have a hose ready, the water running, then you set fire to the moss. It's so dry it goes up in a flash. Then you hose down the tree. It doesn't hurt the tree."

"We discovered that quite by accident," Merritt said, "one Fourth of July when Taylor was fooling with a Roman candle. He set fire to," she looked around for a minute, and then pointed, "that tree."

"Why are they called *live* oaks?" Lisa asked her.

"Because they never die."

"They're evergreens," Taylor cut in. "They have leaves all year."

Outside the park's wooden fence magnolias towered wild in the woods, and giant dogwoods stretched their extensive wings in among the pines. In the early spring, Merritt said, the woods soared with broad intersecting planes of pink and white. Now its dense greenness looked impenetrable. Lisa drooped against the fence. It had been her idea to walk down to the bottom of the park, but she was suddenly exhausted, even though they'd been moving slowly, and was drenched with sweat, as if someone had thrown a wet Hudson's Bay blanket over her. She was having trouble breathing.

"We'll see the lake tomorrow," Merritt said, eyeing Lisa's Italian sandals, "when you're properly shod."

Back on the gallery, famished, not having eaten since breakfast, Lisa joined Merritt in yet another bourbon and watched the moon come up from behind the lake, or fish pond, as Taylor called it. Taylor, who wasn't drinking now, took a small plastic bag from his pocket and rolled a joint. Lisa's eyes widened, but his mother appeared not to notice. She did, though, hold out a hand to stop him when he went to light it.

"Would you mind going in for my cigarettes first? I left them on the hall table." Taylor got to his feet, grudgingly.

"I can't believe you're still smoking."

She looked up at him. "What possible good would it do to quit now?" When he still hesitated, she dropped her voice to an even lower register. "Taylor, I've been sneaking around my own house like a criminal for months—first your sister, and now you—and I'm not going to do it anymore. How many times have I stood aside and let you be a damn fool?" When he had gone inside, she turned to Lisa. "I assume Taylor has told you."

Lisa nodded, her eyes on a small lizard that had appeared at the top of the steps, darting its head from side to side. Taylor had also told her that his mother had refused chemotherapy, preferring not to waste what time she had left in such unpleasant activity. The lizard moved twice, like two rapid blinks of an eye, toward Lisa's chair. Under its chin a large red bubble expanded and contracted.

"Where is it?" Lisa asked, after a minute. "I mean, is it lung cancer?"

Merritt waved an airy hand, as if indicating a rapidly growing ground cover. "Oh. It's everywhere."

LISA PROPPED HERSELF ON an elbow and took the mug of coffee Taylor held out to her. He cocked his head to the side.

"Are you all right?"

She eyed him sadly, her voice heavy with remorse. "I didn't even know we had seafood until I threw it up." He sat on the edge of the bed.

"You threw up? When?"

"I don't know. I couldn't find my watch. Don't worry. I found the bathroom." She took a sip of coffee. "So did a horsefly. It stayed right with me the whole time."

"You don't remember the gumbo? You said it was the most wonderful thing you'd ever eaten."

"I don't remember anything after sitting down at the table. Do you always eat at midnight?"

"You're just used to eating with the kids."

"It was ten o'clock before anyone even mentioned dinner. I remember you pouring the wine, and then nothing, until this helicopter landed in my ear."

"Why didn't you wake me up?"

"There wasn't time." She handed him the mug and sank back against the pillows. Her eyes traveled hesitantly around the room. She didn't want to ask how she got here, to this bed, how she got undressed. Her open suitcase was on the hearth, its contents spilled everywhere. She sighed, dragging her voice to its feet like some shamed thing.

"I'll never be able to face your mother again."

"Why?" He seemed genuinely surprised. "You were fine.

I didn't even know you were in trouble until we came up here. I was trying to catch that horsefly and my mother said, 'You'd better catch your friend first.' You just sort of folded."

"You'd better tell me everything."

He sat on the edge of the bed and smiled down at the floor. "Well. When the moon lit up the last of the magnolia blossoms, you were sure it was a big white star in the sky, and you wouldn't hear otherwise."

"Oh, God." Lisa passed a hand over her face. "I actually remember that part."

"We should have fed you sooner. I shouldn't have let you drink all that bourbon. You were probably dehydrated already from the heat. I shouldn't have given you that joint." He held out the coffee to her again. "But when you want to do something, you're not easy to stop."

She drank the rest of the coffee in silence, absorbing the details of the room, which was the entire width of the house. Four large windows opened onto the park side and, directly across from them, French windows stood open to a screened sleeping porch, lined with cots. In the ceiling overhead was set a large medallion of carved leaves.

"This is a beautiful room. Is it yours?"

"Yes," he said, and then laughed. "You didn't like it much last night. You said it gave you the creeps. You said this whole house gave you the creeps. You said it was a spooky old house and you didn't want to sleep here."

"Oh, my God. Did your mother hear me?"

"I don't think so." He stretched out next to her on the bed. "I had my hand over your mouth."

"WE'RE DESCENDED FROM PIRATES. Did Taylor tell you that?" Leading the way from the kitchen to the gallery, Merritt paused in the hallway. From both walls a constellation of somber, vaguely familiar faces glimmered faintly.

"Well, from one pirate really. He ran away from his family in Normandy at the age of fifteen and went to sea. The legend is that he didn't know he'd shipped with pirates until it was too late, but that he quickly acquired a taste for that way of life. Sometime during the first five years of the nineteenth century he arrived in New Orleans with a fortune. He took the name of Van France and bought himself a blue-blooded wife. Then he came upriver looking for land. He bought six hundred thousand acres from the Choctaws, with a ship's hold full of pig iron."

"Pig iron? What could Indians do with pig iron?"

"Nothing, of course. I imagine he knew it would be useless to them. But then he *was* a pirate. He bought five hundred West Indian slaves to clear the land, and to plant it. He's not here." She glanced around as if she might have seen him a moment ago.

"But there's his son. And there's *his* son, Franklin. He's the one who bought all those horses you took such a fancy to in the dining room your first night." In the dining room motion portraits were whimsically arranged so that the horses appeared to gallop down one wall and up the other. Lisa did not remember having taken a fancy to them.

"He went to the continent every spring, while his money lasted, and brought back the finest thoroughbreds he could find. He hired traveling portrait painters to do every one of them in oils. There's his wife, Emily."

In the wedge of bright morning light angling into the hall, Merritt's olive skin was drained and gray, and the dark brown patches beneath her eyes had a layered look, as if sleeplessness had left its mark night after night for months. Taylor had told Lisa, but it was only now, seeing her in relation to those whose ranks she was about to join, that she fully realized Merritt was dying.

"She was from Massachusetts." Merritt stepped aside to let Lisa take a closer look at the plump young woman with bare shoulders, whose unhappy dark eyes met hers.

"Franklin married her while he was still at Harvard. But she wouldn't come back here with him when he took his degree. He came back alone. His uncle was scandalized. *He* went after her. *He* persuaded her to come."

"She doesn't look very happy about it," Lisa said.

"No, I don't suppose she *was*."

"WHAT'S WRONG, TAYLOR?"

Lisa had found him, as she had at the end of every other day for the past two weeks, sitting alone at the far end of the gallery in a wide wicker chair, his head back, arms motionless on the armrests, eyes fixed on some point in the distance she couldn't identify. He put out a hand and drew her down to the armrest, where she sat facing him. He'd been working with Samson every day, building a porch onto the back of Samson's house, and his face was deeply tanned. His eyes, by contrast, seemed to have lightened a shade. Their blueness always took her by surprise.

"You've been sleeping again." He traced a quilt pattern on her cheek with a forefinger.

"I can't seem to stay awake in the afternoon. I don't know how you function in this heat. I feel stunned."

"You get used to it. Your blood thins out."

She raised her eyebrows. "After how many generations?"

"I've been thinking." He paused. "I've been thinking about putting in air conditioning."

"Is that what you've been thinking about?"

His eyes slid away again and she could see, if not what he was seeing, at least what he was looking at, reflected in the watery glass of the long window behind his chair: the darkening lawn and trees, the lake beyond filled with yellow light. She got up and pulled another chair closer to his. They sat in silence for a while before she spoke again.

"You're not coming back, are you?"

He shifted his eyes to the middle distance, but didn't look at her. "I can't leave now."

"I don't mean now," she said, carefully. "I mean later."

From somewhere nearby a whippoorwill called, and then again, and again. Taylor raised himself out of the chair with one swift movement and walked to the top of the steps, where he stood leaning his shoulder against a support post. After a minute, he held out his hand to her.

"I want to show you something, while there's still light."

He led her around to the back of the house and shouldered open the door of the first of the outbuildings, the one Merritt had told her had been the cook's house. Merritt had showed her inside all of the buildings. This one, with a two-sided fireplace in the middle and four small murky windows, was crowded with glass-topped display counters from some Van France's haberdashery store somewhere, sometime. There was a monstrous mirrored armoire backed up against one side of the fireplace, and a dozen torn cane-bottomed chairs stacked on top of each other, even a hooded wooden infant's cradle. The ceiling was covered with dirt-dauber nests: ugly, gray, chewed-looking things, like papier-mâché model railroad tunnels turned upside down. The gallery ceilings of the house had all been covered with them at one time too, Merritt had told her, until she'd discovered that if you painted a ceiling this particular pale shade of blue, dirt-daubers would mistake it for the sky and wouldn't build their nests against it.

"The Chicagoland of the insect world," Taylor said, following her eyes. "But we can get rid of them easily enough. It's a little dim now, I know, but I could easily cut in a skylight. And a week of steady fires will dry out the damp and must." His voice picked up energy as he envisioned the transformation.

"I'll wire it for electricity, put in an air conditioner, shelves all along that wall. It would make a great studio. It's exactly what you need. We can build a kiln, too. That's something Samson just happens to know a good deal about."

"Taylor." Lisa touched his arm and turned him around to face her. "What are you talking about? Nobody ever said anything about living here."

IT WAS A MUGGY, rainy night in early September when she first met Taylor, who was in Chicago for the opening of his sister's show at the Michigan Avenue gallery owned by Lisa's former husband Welby. Their two daughters, who lived most of the time with Lisa, always spent Friday nights with Welby's parents in Hyde Park, and Lisa was on her way home through a rush-hour downpour to an empty apartment when she passed the gallery. Seeing a party in progress, and drawn by the artist's name, Van France King, on the handsome posters in the window, she went inside. At the time, she was still on very good terms with Welby. It was later, when Taylor moved in with her and the girls, that things with Welby had become strained.

Shaping the air with his hands, Welby was explaining how the materials used alter the space in which a work exists. "These sculptures have little or no supporting armature: they hang from the wall or sit directly on the floor, rendering a pedestal obsolete." He went on to describe the profound sense of play underlying the sculptures, which were constructed from handmade paper and slender pieces of curved blond wood, and their artful combination of texture and form. He spoke with such authority that when he mentioned how one particular sculpture irresistibly invited the viewer's participation, even the artist, a tall, imposing young woman draped in wine-colored cloths, swung around for another look. Lisa, who in her senior year of majoring in art had found Welby's self-assurance irresistible, merely swirled the wine in her glass. When she looked up, all eyes still followed Welby's extended arm, except for Taylor's, blue as the cobalt sky of a fall afternoon, which were watching her.

They ate a late dinner at a restaurant near the gallery and then, unwilling to part, unsure how to proceed, let their coffee cups be refilled so many times that when they finally left the restaurant they were wound up tight enough to walk all night. He wanted to know all about her. She had never met a man who asked so many questions, and who seemed to really want to hear the answers.

When she said that she worked in an art supply store three or four days a week but still thought of herself as a potter, most people left it at that. But Taylor wanted to know how much time she spent at it, where she worked, how many pots she had turned, where he could see some. She detoured him by a jewelry store that had one of her favorite bowls tilted in its window, spilling colorful beads and gold chains, and he said the one right thing without even thinking about it. "Why did they put all that junk in it?"

Pausing on the Michigan Avenue bridge, resting their arms on the railing and looking down into the black water with its bright pools of reflected light, he asked her about Welby: they seemed to get along well enough; why had they broken up? Was it because of one thing, or was it everything?

"It was one thing. And everything," she said. "It was a mistake, from beginning to end."

"I've walked away from some things too," he said, when she didn't elaborate. "That doesn't necessarily make them mistakes."

"This one was." She took a box of restaurant matches from her raincoat pocket and struck one, dropped it down into the river. "It turned out Welby was gay. Is."

"I thought it had to be something like that," Taylor said. "I've been thinking about it."

It wasn't until the next day that he told her about himself: how he'd driven at Bridgehampton, Watkins Glen, Daytona Beach, Mexico City; how he'd always loved cars, loved speed, how he'd caught the auto-racing fever irrevocably when he was a sophomore at Harvard, watching his roommate's father's Maserati do battle with a whole fleet of Ferraris at Sebring, and never went back to school. His friend's father took him on, let him work in the pit, and two years later he was driving himself. It had taken another eleven years for fear, the one thing you could not have and still drive two hundred miles per hour, to catch up with him. Now, he was retired.

"Eleven years," she said, "at two hundred miles an hour."

"I didn't drive twenty-four hours a day," he said. "I had to shift down on hairpins."

"TAYLOR SAID YOU WANT to wait till he come back."

Samson was standing on the edge of the horse lot, where Lisa suspected he'd been on the lookout for her. She and Taylor had planned to ride early, but he'd had to drive his mother into town.

"I'll be all right, Samson. I thought I'd try the Morgan today. He's gentle enough." But the old man shook his head.

"No more gentler than the one threw you the other day."

"She didn't throw me. I fell off. And we were practically standing still. I wasn't hurt." But Samson shook his head again in a stubborn way that maddened Lisa.

"Ask me, there's nothing wrong with that horse a two-by-four upside the head won't cure. But Taylor said you want to wait."

Stiff-legged in Merritt's riding boots, Lisa turned and strode back to the house where she let the screen door slam. After a considerable struggle, which left her soaked with sweat, she managed to pull the boots off and then changed into shorts and sneakers. She had some breakfast, a bowl of yogurt she ate standing in the pool of cold air in front of the open refrigerator door. Then, regretting her rudeness, she went outside again to look for Samson and walked all the way to his house before she found him emerging from a small shed in back, a fishing pole in one hand and a small wire cage in the other.

"I bet them kids of yours like to fish," he said, ignoring her apology. She shook her head.

"They're both girls."

"I know it. I know you got two girls. You telling me girls don't like to fish?" Samson's voice slid incredulously up the scale. "My wife liked to fish. Taylor's little sister likes to fish. We fished nearly every day Van was here. Even *she* likes to fish." Lisa had come to know that when Samson used a female pronoun with no apparent reference, he was referring to Merritt, and in this instance, she was surprised.

"She does?"

"Sure she does. She and Corinne, before Corinne went and died, they liked nothing better than to take them kids fishing." Samson held up his gear, an offering.

"You don't want to go fishing? Thought maybe you could fish instead of riding them fool horses." When she hesitated, not knowing what to say, he shook his head and turned to put back the fishing gear. Then he stopped, reluctant to give up the idea, and held up the little cage made of wire and screen.

"This here. You put your fish in it and let it back down in the water. That way he'll still be alive. And no snake'll get in there either." He laughed. "Corinne. She'd get that mad when a snake'd get her fish. That's why I made her up this box." He turned back to the shed and spoke over his shoulder. "You bring them kids down here, I'll teach 'em to fish. That's what they like. They like to ride and fish and run and holler." He came out and shut and latched the door of the shed. "City's no place to live."

"I guess Taylor's been talking to you," Lisa said, after a minute.

"Sure Taylor's been talking to me. Why wouldn't Taylor be talking to me?" They were standing in a clearing and Lisa, dazed by the sun, passed a hand over her eyes.

"You come to the house," Samson said. "You want you a glass of water or something cool." He turned and walked to his house without waiting for an answer. Lisa followed him inside. After the outdoors it was astonishingly cool. More surprising still were the furnishings. Lisa couldn't resist running an appraising hand over the cold marble surface of a serving table just inside the kitchen door.

"That come from the house," Samson said. "That too." He pointed to a Welsh mirror-backed dresser. While he busied himself rinsing glasses and getting ice and water, he talked steadily.

"I didn't want to take none of it, but she said, 'Samson, don't you turn fool on me now. I got enough stuff stored on this place to fit out six houses and you earned it. You and Corinne earned every bit of it.' She's not like some." He motioned Lisa into a chair and settled himself heavily at the kitchen table.

"And she brought them kids up to do right. Taylor was just a little bitty boy and his sister a baby when their daddy died. Corinne helped her. And I taught that boy how to hunt and fish and take care of himself. He's a good boy. He's been running away from this place all his life. But he's a good boy. That's why he come back."

STANDING JUST INSIDE THE open doorway of Samson's house, the living room door, facing the woods, Lisa watched the two men work on the porch they'd been building. The ceiling fan above the table coaxed a breeze to travel through the door to the open windows behind her and she stood squarely in its path. Outside, Taylor and Samson sweated copiously, Samson's shirt plastered to his back by a wide dark circle.

Taylor had taken his shirt off and tied a rolled cotton scarf around his forehead to keep the sweat out of his eyes. Lisa liked the way his muscles worked so efficiently, expanding and contracting, tightening and relaxing. She liked the way his slim back narrowed down into the wide belt threaded through the loops of his jeans.

He asked her to hand him things: nails, a hammer, the level. Each time, she moved slowly and deliberately. She had come to equate equilibrium with keeping cool. The level fascinated her with its slender glass tubes of greenish liquid. Taylor was using it to position the bottom of the porch railings. When he finished with it she picked it up and stepped back into the path of moving air. She closed her eyes and held the level out in front of her on the flat of her upturned palms, perfectly level, she thought. But when she opened her eyes the air bubble in the tube on the left was way below the one on the right. The game intrigued her. She tried again and again, but couldn't bring both bubbles to rest on center, and wondered if equilibrium, too, was an illusion.

Then Samson, far below the platform of the porch, where the ground sloped steeply away from the house to the stack of lumber from which he was selecting the two-by-four that would be the next rung of the porch railing, gave out a sharp cry. She stepped out onto the platform just as a snake, thick as an arm and yellow-brown with diamonds strewn down its back, curved twice, and twice again, out of sight into the woods.

Taylor was there first, because he jumped from the platform, while she went through the house and around. Samson was on his back, the leg of his overalls shoved up to his knee and Taylor's red scarf already tied tightly around his hairless, coffee-colored calf. Below the tourniquet, two black punctures oozed colorless liquid. Taylor took out his pocketknife and opened it.

"You've got to sit up some, Samson," he said. "Come on. Sit up." But Samson didn't hear. His face was covered with tiny beads of sweat and his eyes were opened wider than seemed possible, the irises shrunk to the size of dried peas and surrounded by red-veined, yellow whites. "Oh Lord, Oh Lord, Oh Lord," he moaned. "Get him up," Taylor said over his shoulder.

Lisa dropped to her knees behind Samson and lifted his head and shoulders. He was a big man but amazingly light, as if old age had begun its erosion from within, hollowing him out. Propping him up against her thighs she could feel his heart fluttering, like a trapped bird. She put both hands on his chest, as if she could calm his heart and stop it from trying to escape.

With his knife, Taylor made two sure, swift incisions, one over each of the punctures. Then he bent over Samson's leg, covered both cuts with his mouth, sucked noisily and spat off to the side. "Taylor!" Lisa cried out. The thought of that venom on his lips, teeth and tongue made her sick with fear. But he did it again and again, sucking the poison out and spitting it contemptuously away. "All right, Samson," he said at last, his voice curiously thick. Sitting back on his heels, he wiped his mouth with the back of his hand. "All right."

"It's the fangs that shoot it into the bloodstream," Taylor told her. "You could drink a gallon of it and get nothing worse than a stomach ache. Even Livy knew that."

"Who's Livy?" Still groggy, Lisa envisioned some former wife, fled back to the city.

"Livy the Roman historian. Second year Latin," he said. "He's got a long passage on it. Samson was in some danger. I was not."

"I couldn't have done that in a million years." Lisa rolled over onto her back on the narrow cot. She'd been sleeping on the porch off Taylor's room, for over two hours, he told her when he came back from taking Samson to the doctor.

"Sure you could. If it was me? If it was one of your children?"

"My children!"

He bent to kiss her, but thinking of the poison that had lately touched his lips, she averted hers at the last minute and took his kiss somewhere behind her left ear. He straightened and looked down at her, moving his head once in mock disbelief. Then he went into his room, and she heard his feet in the hall and on the stairs.

She hadn't told him yet that she'd made her decision, that she would be coming back with the children, to stay. She didn't know exactly what had made up her mind, any more than she knew why the call of the whippoorwill at dusk made her want to weep at the same time it made her want to hear it again and again. It wasn't Taylor's promise of the most ideal studio she could have imagined for herself, or even the considerable lure of the physical beauty of the place she had gradually fallen prey to over the past month. It wasn't the eagerness to be brought here that her own treacherous children expressed every time she and Taylor talked to them on the telephone. Or even the fear of losing Taylor. That was not a question; they both knew that now. Even Samson knew that, that she could make Taylor leave here if she wanted.

"Anybody can stop a man from doing what she knows he ought to do," he'd said to her the day they sat at his kitchen table. "But ain't nobody can stop what happens to him after that." Cowboy talk, she'd told herself, although Samson had made it sound something very like wisdom.

The night she arrived she'd said something about how hard it was to find the house and Merritt had observed, wryly, that

that's why it was still standing. "You Yankees passed us by, didn't even know we were here." "Don't look at me," Lisa had said. "My ancestors were being beaten to death in Europe at the time."

It had something to do with that, she knew, that she had no deep connection to any one spot on earth, not like Taylor's connection to this place, the visceral nature of which she had glimpsed this afternoon watching him suck the poison from Samson's wound. What it came down to was that she was free to move, while he apparently was not. He was tethered so firmly that when he'd tried to run away all he'd been able to do was drive as fast as humanly possible in circles.

From somewhere below she heard the deep cadence of Merritt's voice lifting to drop a question. After a pause she heard Taylor's response. She knew she should get downstairs. She knew Merritt looked forward to the cocktail hour, and it was getting dark now. But she stayed where she was. Inertia had taken possession of her, moving through her bloodstream like a poison, turning it sluggish. Lying on her back, looking up at the dirt-dauber blue ceiling, she thought of all she had to do. She'd moved many times in her life, but always within the Chicago city limits. She could hardly bear to contemplate even the drive back there, now that she knew just how far away she was, just how far south. If she left right now, she thought—if she could find her way out of here—and drove straight north all night, she'd probably still be in Mississippi.

A Complicated Situation

"Did Barbara ever tell you *our* story?" Horace, speaking to Barbara's husband Jack, reaches over to put his arm around Barbara's sister Mags and gives her shoulder a little squeeze. "How their father tried to kill me?"

"And how you saved his life," Mags adds.

Surprised, Jack glances at Barbara, who says it's true that Horace, who was by the time of her father's first heart attack a cardiologist with his own practice in Chicago, once saved her father's life, or at least caused him to live several years more after another doctor had actually given him up for dead, but it's not true that her father had once tried to kill Horace; he simply, in his anger at seeing Horace at a particular moment, lost control of the car.

"You weren't there," Mags says to Barbara, in her deep, emphatic voice. "Daddy deliberately tried to run Horace down." She turns to Jack. "Can you imagine? My own father trying to make my son an orphan on the day he was born?"

"I was coming out of the hospital. I had to flatten myself against the wall." Horace gets up to demonstrate, flinging his arms back melodramatically. Before he can sit down again, the beeper in his pocket sounds. He excuses himself and goes out to the front hall to call his answering service.

"It was a very narrow walled driveway." For Jack's benefit, Barbara describes the entrance to the hospital in the western Massachusetts town where she and Mags grew up. "It was narrow and curved and uphill. There were so many accidents they finally had to dismantle it and put in a new entrance."

"What are you talking about, accidents?" Mags says. "You know Daddy wanted to kill Horace. He wanted to kill me too." She turns to Jack again. "He smashed my picture. He broke it over his knee and threw it against the wall."

"He took it out of the frame first," Barbara says. "Then he tore it up. He didn't smash anything. He didn't throw anything against the wall."

It was Mags's high school graduation photograph and had sat for three years in its silver frame among the others on top of the piano in the living room. Barbara's father destroyed it, tearing it into tiny shreds, the night he was told that Mags had eloped with Horace. The day he allegedly tried to hit Horace with his car was nearly seven months later, the day he suddenly realized that Mags must have been pregnant when she eloped. Mags is lumping the two events together because she is a little drunk. They all are, except Horace, who has been slyly filling his champagne glass with ice water.

"This is incredible," Jack says. "I can't believe what you're telling me." His eyes travel the room, up to the intricately molded ceiling with its Grecian medallion in the center, from which hangs a fairly magnificent chandelier; down the length of several richly patterned Persian rugs, to the stone fireplace, big enough to walk into. Barbara knows what he is thinking: a bit rich for his taste, but who would think this wasn't good enough for his daughter?

He and Barbara were just telling Horace and Mags some retrospectively amusing anecdotes about the difficulties they had encountered some years before in extracting themselves from their former marriages, and Barbara told Jack that, difficult as things had actually been, they would have been worse still if her parents had been alive at the time. She told Jack that if her parents had been alive, she would probably never have married him; she wouldn't have had the courage to leave her first husband. Mags had nodded her confirmation, and then Horace had said what he'd said about telling *their* story. Now Barbara is sorry. She wants Jack to think well of her parents, who after all have been dead for seventeen years.

"If it wasn't for them," Mags once said, when she was telling Barbara about some rumors she had heard concerning Horace and one of the nurses at the hospital, "I'd leave him so fast." Barbara had known that "them" meant her parents, not Mags's and Horace's children, all boys, who were two, three, four, and five years old at the time. "I wouldn't give them the satisfaction. But, boy, as soon as they're gone . . ."

Yet, when both of their parents died not four years later, prematurely and within six weeks of each other, Mags did not leave Horace. They seemed to be getting along fine then and they had already bought this house, with its lake views and tennis court, in one of the posh suburbs some distance upshore from the city. Horace had a Porsche, and for family outings there was first the wood-paneled station wagon and then the extravagantly equipped van, a recreation room on wheels. There is no longer a van, as the boys all have their own cars. It's Mags who has a Porsche now, and Horace has recently bought a midnight blue Jaguar that he tends with great care and affection.

Barbara remembers one hot summer afternoon when she and Mags were little girls, lying on the cool floor of the guest room, looking at a magazine left behind by one of their uncles. Mags was fascinated by a photograph, a car ad, of a woman in a filmy white gown, on the balcony of some tropical mansion, watching a man in a white dinner jacket step into a sleek car parked on the moonlit gravel below. She kept coming back to the picture, again and again, and later cut it out to hang on her bedroom wall. Barbara was equally attracted to a whiskey ad picturing a thoughtful-looking man in a tweed jacket, smoking a pipe in a library of leather-bound books, a glass of amber liquid at his leather-patched elbow. In a way, she thinks now, they have both gotten what they said they wanted that day. There are no leather patches, or leather bindings for that matter, but there are thousands of books, and Barbara's husband does smoke a pipe, although only one a day now and always outdoors, and teaches English in a northeastern university, as she does herself.

THERE IS A MUFFLED pop far away in the kitchen, and soon Paul moves swiftly into the dining room, where his elders are grouped at one end of the mahogany table strewn with useless gifts of silver, although the invitations had specified, "No presents, please. Just your presence." With a white linen napkin draped over a white-shirted forearm, he triumphantly holds up a spuming bottle of champagne. "Look what I found. We thought it was all gone."

Barbara watches admiringly as her nephew, the bottle resting on his forearm, like a waiter, refills their glasses: hers first, then his mother's, then Jack's. Paul is twenty-four and incredibly handsome. Like his three brothers, in conjunction with whom he has given the silver wedding anniversary party that has just ended, he has achieved the best possible combination of his parents' genes: his Japanese father's neat, trim body, rich coloring, and hair so black it shines, as if polished; his mother's large green eyes, full mouth, flawless complexion, her highly expressive arrangement of features.

"No. None for me," Horace says, coming back to the table as Paul is about to fill his glass. "I have to go." Paul bows in a waiterly fashion—his father's having to leave in the middle of family gatherings is something he is as accustomed to as breathing—and retreats to the kitchen where he and his brothers are sitting around another table, drinking other things and watching a movie, relaxing after cleaning up the worst of the mess from their party.

"I thought you got Sam to cover for you today." Disappointment (or is it suspicion?) gives an edge to Mags's voice. Horace gets up and stands behind her chair, his small, elegant hands on her shoulders. Mags, who is still quite pretty, used to be thin, small and petite, a perfect match for Horace, who plays tennis nearly every day, still has the flat body of a boy, and is fastidious about his appearance.

"I have a patient in ICU who won't be there tomorrow," he says. "I have to see him. I have to see his family." He kisses the top of Mags's head, gently, with such affection that it's difficult for Barbara to imagine him having an affair with another woman. Not that she ever doubted that what Mags told her was true.

"This is an emergency," Horace says to Mags. "I have to go." But apparently not yet, because after a moment's hesitation he sits back down at the table.

"I remember when I came to tell your parents that I wanted to marry Mags," Horace is speaking to Barbara now. "You opened the door. You looked so scared."

"*You* looked scared," she counters. "I was just surprised." She remembers how she flung open the door, expecting someone else, and found Horace on the doorstep, his hands joined together, as if in prayer, his body already bending towards her in a formal bow.

THERE HAD BEEN RUMORS. In 1962 an Asian was still conspicuous in that town in western Massachusetts, especially if he had

his arm around a young white woman. Horace, just recently
arrived from Japan, was an intern. Mags had graduated from
nursing school that May. She had a room in the nurses' dormi-
tory attached to the hospital but still kept most of her clothes
and other belongings in her room at home, where she usually
spent several nights a week.

She was seen with Horace in a restaurant, in front of a theatre, in a car. People would tell Barbara's mother, or Barbara, but
neither Barbara nor her mother—nor anyone else, for that
matter—dared mention it to Barbara's father. Questioned by
her mother, Mags would say that Horace was just a good friend,
or that he was lonely, he didn't know many people in this
country, she felt sorry for him. Her mother would always say,
"Mags, if your father finds out about this . . ."

Then they were seen in Boston together one weekend, and
there was a scene between Mags and her mother. Mags was
sullen and stubborn, silent. Their mother stormed: What if she
ended up married to this person and he took her to Japan to
live? What if he brought his whole family over here to live with
them? What if he expected her to behave like a geisha girl? Just
how much did Mags know about him?

Barbara was not there; she was waiting in her room until she
heard the front door slam. Then she went down to the living
room, where her mother, who had been crying, described the
scene to her. Mags didn't know a thing about this person, she
said, about his background or his family or his country, his cul-
ture, his customs. And she didn't want to know; she didn't care.

Barbara's mother called the director of the nursing school,
a motherly woman who had always taken an interest in Mags
and who said that she had just been about to call *her*. She said
that Mags's and Dr. Kiuchi's romance was no secret and that
everyone in the hospital, from the chief of staff to the janitorial
staff, was shocked and scandalized. Summoned home again the

next night for another talk, Mags said it was not true that everyone at the hospital was scandalized. She and Horace had many friends; other interns and residents had invited them home for dinner, and her own friends were all crazy about Horace. After this session Barbara remained in her room. Her mother, she later learned, went down to the garage at the back of the yard, shut the doors, stuffed the space beneath them with rags, and screamed.

A day or two later there came a letter from Horace addressed to Barbara's parents. Her mother showed Barbara the letter, but she did not show it to Barbara's father. It was long and formally expressed, written on onionskin paper in an elegant, spidery hand. Horace introduced himself and said he wished to marry their daughter and their daughter wished to marry him, too, but refused, out of fear, to bring him to her home to meet her parents so that he might ask their permission. Therefore he was presuming to address them himself; he was seeking an interview. He would like to speak to them as soon as possible. He gave an address and two telephone numbers. Would they please contact him?

After reading his letter, Barbara's mother thought that if she never contacted Horace, he would never come, that he would not come without being invited. She also thought that, no matter what Mags was willing to do, Horace was the kind of man who would not marry her without her parents' blessing.

Barbara wasn't so sure. Horace had taken Mags to Boston for a weekend, hadn't he? What if they were in too deep for a polite good-bye? In the volumes of Japanese literature her mother had checked out of the library recently, Barbara had read several love stories that ended with the lovers committing suicide together. She had read that this was the subject of many Kabuki plays, couples committing suicide, which the Japanese were said to regard as an effective means of redeeming one's honor and bringing a complicated situation to an end. But all she said to her mother was that Horace seemed like a very nice person, if his letter was any indication.

"Your sister would never be able to adapt," Barbara's mother told her. "I know what she's thinking, if she's thinking at all. She's thinking that this person wants to be an American. He's told her that, that he wants to live here for the rest of his life. But, believe me, he won't become more like us as he gets older. He'll become more and more Japanese. People revert more and more the older they get. She thinks she can cut him loose from all his connections, that she can gradually chip away at all the things that are different about him, things she doesn't like, until he becomes just like her. She has no intention of making any concessions herself. Believe me, I know Mags. She doesn't know where Japan is. She won't even bother to look it up on a map."

Barbara thought a lot about all of this. What was to stop any man—no matter how well you knew him or how much he was like you—from changing later? Her mother and father had grown up in the same town; they were engaged for six years; they had, presumably, known all that could be learned about each other. Yet, if Barbara's father had gradually turned into an Eskimo, a Laplander, a Zulu, he could hardly be more different now from the man—cheerful, fun-loving, fabulous dancer—her mother claimed to have married twenty-some years before.

No. No matter what reasons her mother gave, the real one was racism. (Prejudice was the word used then.) Her mother simply did not want her daughter to marry a Japanese. Barbara had overheard some of the things her mother had said to Mags, things she had not repeated later to Barbara. She had asked Mags to think what it would be like never to set foot in her home again, never to see her family again, because, believe her, that's what marrying this person would mean. She asked her to imagine being handed her first child and looking down at a foreigner, a Japanese baby with slanty eyes. She asked her to imagine being the mother of a whole family of Japanese children. She asked her to think about Barbara, how she was ruining not only her own but her sister's chances of "making a good marriage."

Barbara's own feeling on this subject was that if having a Japanese brother-in-law would keep someone from marrying her, she would be very grateful to Horace for eliminating such a person ahead of time. She was already quite well disposed toward him, although extremely surprised, the day she leapt down the stairs to open the door, expecting her friend Diane, and instead found Horace, who had no doubt been expecting one of Mags's parents to open the door, already bowing to her. He was so slight, so young, so handsome. Barbara wanted to take his hand and run away, to help him escape from the ugly Americans inside. What would her father do? He hadn't even been told yet. Horace had no idea, but her father didn't even know that Horace existed. Stunned, she simply stood there, staring. The young Japanese doctor smiled faintly, bravely. "Haro," she thought he said.

"YOU THINK YOU WERE surprised," Horace says, then laughs. "You should have seen your father."

Barbara had not seen him. She told Horace to wait at the door while she went to tell her parents someone wanted to see them. Then she pointed the way to the living room and made her own escape, outside and down to the end of the street. She wanted to head Diane off at the pass; she didn't want her to hear whatever there might be to hear. While she waited she prayed, she crossed her fingers. She hoped Horace would not bow to her father. She hoped he would not say, "Haro."

"What did he say?" Jack asks Horace. "Their father."

"He say (Horace still slips into present tense at times, as if he thinks the verb in an answer should echo the verb in a question) he will kill me. He will kill both of us. He told me to get out of his house."

"What did you say? Did you leave?"

"Not right away. Their mother looked nice. She was nice. So I tried to say what I planned." He looks at Mags, a little wistfully, a former Horace looking at a former Mags. "That I love her so much."

"How did you feel?" Jack was a newspaper reporter before he went back to graduate school. He often asks a question where another man might not. "Were you afraid?"

"Oh, sure. He's threatening me." Horace reaches for Mags's glass and takes a sip of champagne, then replaces the glass. He laughs, almost fondly, remembering. "Joe was a big man then, before all the heart trouble. Big voice. When I watched baseball with him, I watched him. When Joe's happy, I'm happy. When Joe's mad, I'm mad. When Joe jumps up and yells, I jump up and yell. So he tricks me. Nothing is happening, but he yells. So I yell: yea, rah, rah. Then he looks at me. He says, What the hell are *you* yelling about?"

"You watched baseball together?" Jack asks, when he stops laughing. "How did that come about?" Jack is a passionate baseball fan. He's always thought that Barbara's father would have liked him because of that, that they would have gotten along. But Jack was married when Barbara met him; in her father's book, that would have been worse than being Japanese.

"It was football," Mags says. "You were watching football. It was Thanksgiving."

"That's right," Horace says. "First football, then baseball."

"But you were watching football when that happened." Mags turns to Jack. "We were allowed to come home about two months after we were married. It was Thanksgiving. My mother got my father to agree to let us come for dinner. She invited a priest too, just to be on the safe side."

The dinner had not gone too badly. Mags's father, although he didn't volunteer a single remark beyond the observation that Mags was getting "fat," had too much respect for his pastor not to respond when spoken to, and Rev. Vaughn did his valiant best to keep the conversation going. But once he was gone, her father disappeared into the television room and turned on a football game. Horace, feeling that his place was with the man of the house, moved silently into the room and sat in a chair placed slightly behind his father-in-law's. Later, Mags and Barbara crept to the doorway to look. They gasped and held on to each other when Horace jumped out of his chair and shouted, "Goddamn stupid ape!" just after their father had done the same.

"When did you get married?" Jack asks Horace. "I mean, how long was it after you first went to see their parents?" Horace looks to Mags for help.

"Five days," she supplies for him. "You went to the house on Sunday. We eloped on Friday. I went home and packed up all my stuff and moved it over to the hospital. Then we drove to Boston. We already had the license."

"How did you move out without anybody noticing?"

"Only Barbara was home." Mags laughs. "She was in the bathroom the *entire* time. She didn't notice a thing."

"I heard you," Barbara says. "I knew what you were doing."

THE DAY MAGS MOVED out, she told Barbara that she was cleaning her room, that she had the afternoon off but was on duty that night. When Barbara heard the closet doors slide back and forth, back and forth, and heard Mags's moving around in the attic overhead, she knew she was leaving for good. Not wanting to see, Barbara stayed in the bathroom. Three years earlier, when Mags was given a set of luggage for Christmas, Barbara had been weepy all day thinking about Mags going away to college, never coming back, things never being the same again. Then Mags decided on nursing school and, since there was a good one right there, had in effect stayed home another few years. But that did not make it any easier to see her go now. Barbara dried her hair, shaved her legs, even did her nails. At last Mags came to the door and called, "So long, Barbara. I've got to go to work." Barbara called back, cheerily enough, "Bye, Mags," then covered her face with a towel and wept.

She waited until after dinner to go into her sister's room and look in the empty drawers and closets. While she was there, her mother came into the room. Her appearance changed alarmingly, her color a deadly white with bright pink spots high on her cheeks, her hair actually standing out slightly from her head. Barbara thought she would have a stroke, but her mother went to the telephone and called the hospital. She had Mags paged. She had to a wait a long time, and while she waited she began to cry. She handed the phone to Barbara and shut herself in the bathroom. After another wait a man came on and introduced himself as the chaplain. He thought he was speaking to Mags's mother; he said, "I was going to call on you and your husband this evening. Mags asked me to speak to you." Barbara asked him if it was true Mags had eloped with Dr. Kiuchi. "Yes," he said, relieved she was taking it so calmly. "I'm afraid it is. Mags asked me to tell you. That's why I was coming to see you tonight."

"This is Mags's sister," Barbara said. "I think you'd better come right now."

The chaplain was there within minutes, looking afraid and unhappy, but he went resolutely into the living room where Barbara's father sat reading the newspaper. It hadn't occurred to

Barbara what the effect on him might be, having this somber stranger, clearly the bearer of bad tidings, ushered into his living room, hat in hand. Her father's color, too, drained rapidly away, the newspaper slipped from his hands. "Mags?" he choked on the name. "Is it Mags?" He thought she was dead and that this functionary in black had been sent to break the news.

Thinking that things could only go uphill from there, Barbara went to get her mother. But by the time they returned to the living room her father was shouting that by God he wished Mags *was* dead and that if he ever got his hands on that sneaky little Jap he would kill him. "Did you marry them? Did you?" He looked as if he wanted to kill the chaplain too. Barbara ran out of the house. Behind her, her mother cried, "Joe! Joe!"

Barbara ran up the hill to get Harold Wolfe, a psychologist whose children she often babysat for, and explained as best she could as she hurried him down the street. The chaplain, livid with anger, was getting into his car. Inside the house, Barbara's father, his back to them, was rooting through the front-hall closet, her mother standing behind him, still crying, "Joe! Joe!" For a second Barbara had the feeling of having walked into a cartoon: her father furiously hurling things over his shoulder, her mother standing aside wringing her hands, the most ludicrous expression on her face. But it was only for a second. It was not funny. Her father was looking for his shotgun.

Harold later pointed out to Barbara that the fact that her father had to search for his old squirrel gun—in the front-hall closet, no less—was an indication of how little danger there was he would actually shoot someone with it. Nevertheless, he coaxed her father out of the closet and into a chair. He stood next to him, a firm hand on his shoulder, holding him down, talking to him. Then, when he had him almost calm, he did what seemed to Barbara a lunatic thing: he walked over to the piano and took down Mags's graduation photograph and examined it. Her father sprang out of his chair and snatched it from him. Shaking violently, he slid away the back of the frame, took out Mags's picture, and ripped it to shreds. Then he sat down again and wept helplessly.

Harold told Barbara to get some brandy for her father, then had to send her up to his house for some; her parents did not drink and there was rarely anything in the house. Her father drank a little of the brandy; her mother took a sip too. Soon they went up to bed, walking up the stairs together, side by side, like two children afraid of the dark.

Barbara asked Harold why he had called attention to Mags's picture. "To reduce the pressure," he said. "To allow him to vent his rage in some harmless way, which is what he was doing in that closet. He's through now. He won't hurt your sister or anyone else." Barbara followed him outside when he left. They stood on the front lawn talking, draped around by curtains of white birch leaves. Harold gave her some pointers on how to handle her father in the morning; her mother too. Then he put his hands on Barbara's shoulders and turned her so he could scrutinize her face by the glow of the porch light. "And how about you?" he said. "How's Barbara?"

Her sister gone, her parents greatly diminished, her home life destroyed—or so she thought—Barbara started to cry. Harold put his arms around her and hugged her, just for a second, then kissed her on the forehead. He told her that, although it seemed impossible now, although it seemed life would never be normal again, some day she and Mags would look back on this together and smile. They might even laugh.

HAROLD WAS RIGHT. THEY are all laughing now.

But their mother had been right too, about one thing. Mags had never wanted to make any concessions to cultural differences. Quite the opposite; they aroused her hostility, even little things, like rice. She cooked rice every day because Horace insisted, but, not having been brought up eating it, she cooked it grudgingly, resentfully. Then she bought a rice cooker. She'd get it going every morning and then not have to think about it anymore. If Horace suddenly decided to come home for lunch, and whenever he got around to eating dinner, he could help himself to the rice in the cooker, which by dinnertime was a solid glutinous mass. Mags never ate it herself and never fed it to her children, who were given potatoes instead, or spaghetti; anything but rice.

And there was the question of baths. Not since childhood had Mags taken a bath in the evening; she was a morning shower person. Horace bathed every evening when he got home. The idea of getting into bed unwashed, with gritty feet, had been revolting to him from the start, although they were married four years before he could bring himself to speak of it to Mags. He asked her to bathe in the evening. Perhaps they could bathe together. Mags refused, "in no uncertain terms," she told Barbara, when relating the incident.

There had been other problems. Horace did have a large family; their visits were necessarily lengthy. And Horace would not help Mags at all. He did not feel it was his place to have anything to do with the management of the house, or with the physical care of his children, for whom, when they were very small, a very weary Mags would have to get a babysitter just to run out to the grocery store. But Mags and Horace did not actually separate, and then only for a couple of weeks, until they had been married fifteen years.

Around that time, Mags brought the three younger boys to stay with Barbara in the northeastern college town where she and her first husband were already having their own problems. Paul's soccer team had made it to tournament semifinals, so he

stayed with his father. Horace had promised to be home every
night, apparently something he had not been doing for a couple
of months. But the first night Mags and the younger boys were
at Barbara's, Paul called his mother at eleven-thirty to say his
father was not home yet and he was getting worried.

Mags told Barbara that for several years Horace had been
staying out at least one night a week, and once was gone for an
entire weekend. She knew who it was, "a tiny blond in the
office, who thinks Horace hung the goddamn moon." She
paced up and down the living room with her gin and tonic, getting madder and madder as she talked, until she was almost
shouting. Barbara kept trying to calm her down; she talked and
calmed and soothed and suggested things Mags might say to
Horace. When Mags went upstairs to the bathroom, Barbara's
husband, who had been working in his study off the living room
and had heard every word, came suddenly into the living room.
White around the gills, his thin lips set, compressed, he hissed,
"Why don't you just shut up? She has every right to be mad. Let
her. Let her shout. Sometimes anger and disappointment have
to be expressed, Barbara." Then he went back into his study and
shut the door without a sound. The way he said her name, the
way he'd come in and out so swiftly, silently, made her feel she'd
been bitten by a snake. When Mags came downstairs, she sat
next to Barbara on the sofa and put her arm around her. "I'm
sorry I upset you." She smoothed Barbara's hair back from her
eyes. "I'll be all right, Barbara. Don't worry."

So it was Barbara and her husband who got divorced.
Mags and Horace stayed together without Mags taking any of
Barbara's advice.

On her sister's twenty-sixth wedding anniversary, a year
after the silver anniversary party, Barbara, who has forgotten to

send a card, tries all day to reach her by phone, but there's no answer. Finally, later that night Mags answers, sounding as if she has a terrible cold.

"Oh, it's you. I was afraid this was going to be Horace."

"What do you mean? Where is he?"

"I don't know. With his little blond, I guess."

Barbara is genuinely surprised, having thought that affair long over with—that was ten years ago—having thought Horace and Mags as happy since then as any other long-married couple. Happier. "You mean he's still seeing her?"

There is a long pause before Mags says, "Oh. I see what you mean. No. This is a different one. This one is even younger. This one is the same age as his son for God's sake."

"Mags." Barbara moves the phone away from her desk where stacks of ungraded papers lay waiting. She moves to a more comfortable chair. "Oh, Mags. I'm so sorry."

"And dumb! She's so stupid she tried to back out of the garage at the office without opening the door. And you should *hear* her. She's pure trash."

"You know her?"

"Of course I know her. She works in the office. Where else would Horace meet anyone? Except the hospital. Where else does he go?" Then Mags grows philosophical. "One thing I've learned being married to Horace is that Orientals can't tell the difference between us. We all sound exactly the same to them."

"Mags, I don't believe this."

"You haven't heard anything yet."

Then Mags tells Barbara about meeting Horace after work one night for dinner. She has often gone into Chicago to meet him for dinner, but this dinner was rather romantic. He gave her a beautiful bracelet. He told her he loved her and that she was irreplaceable. She wanted to believe him. Like anyone else, she wants to be loved.

"But he looks so guilty," she says, "as if he's in pain. So naturally I'm suspicious. Then, on the way home, he's following me and I'm trying to keep him in my rearview mirror. But he's driving so slow. I slow down and then he slows down even more. It's raining, really hard, but this is a man who's only happy driving a hundred miles an hour and he's going thirty. On the expressway. It's clear he's trying to lose me. And sure enough. I see him drop way back and sneak off the exit before ours. You won't believe this."

"What? You followed him?"

"How could I follow him? He was behind me. No. I went home. What else could I do? And I knew if I confronted him he'd just say he had a patient, he'd gotten a call on his beeper or something. So I started looking. I just started looking around. I went through everything. He's not so smart himself, you know. On one of his American Express bills in his desk I found a charge for twelve hundred dollars from Field's. I called the credit office. They were still open and I called them and asked about this charge. I had to talk to the night credit manager before I got any information, but she said it was for this bed that we'd ordered. A bed! You like symbolism. There's symbolism for you. So I said yes we'd ordered a bed but we hadn't received it; maybe it went to the wrong address. The whole thing took about an hour from the time I got home.

"So I drive there, ninety miles an hour through this blinding rain. I knock on the door and she answers, and she's scared. She's terrified of me. I didn't tell you this but when I first heard about this one I went to the office. I walked into the waiting room and sat down right across from her and just looked at her. After about three minutes she got up and ran out crying. So I knew. She was the one. So she opens the door and says, 'Oh, Mrs. Kiuchi. This isn't a good time for us to talk.' I say, 'I don't want to talk to you. I want to talk to my husband.'

"Just then Horace wanders around the corner to see who it is. He's got a drink in his hand and his shoes are off. That got me more than anything else, him coming to the door that way in his socks. And he invites me in. He's shocked, he's scared out of his mind, but he invites me in. So I go in, and the place is furnished from my own attic. My old drapes on the windows, my pillows on the sofa, my pictures on the wall. I walk over to one of the pictures and I say, 'I really like this one. Do you mind telling me where you got it?' She runs off to the bedroom and slams the door. Horace looks at me and he says, cold as ice, 'Why did you come here?' I said, 'I came to take a look at that new bed we bought, but I guess it's occupied.' No reaction. No expression. Nothing. So I got really mad. 'Actually,' I said, 'I just came to tell you that when you come home you'll find all of your clothes out in the driveway.'" Mags stops then, as if for breath, as if trying to think how to tell the rest of the story.

"Are you there, Barbara? Do you think you could give some indication that you've heard what I said?"

"I'm just stunned, that's all," Barbara says. "Then what happened?"

"What do you think? Then I went home and threw all of his clothes out in the driveway."

"In the rain?"

"Yes, in the rain."

"Did you throw them out a window? Or did you go up and down?" Barbara knows Horace's things are all up on the third floor, where he has a small office and a larger room to house his significant wardrobe.

"I wish I'd thought of throwing them out the window. No. I went up and down. I went up and down those stairs so many times I nearly had a heart attack. But I got every blessed silk shirt and tie, every cashmere sweater, wool suit, jacket, bathrobe, his camel hair coat, all those expensive Italian shoes.

I got his underwear and pajamas and slippers, his shoe polishing machine and nail clippers and shaving kit, even his toothbrush, and I threw them all out in the driveway. Then I went back for the goddamn rice cooker and threw that on top of everything else. Then I locked the doors and went to bed. No, wait. First I emptied out his desk drawers into cartons and packed them in the trunk of my car."

"But why? Why would you put them in your car?"

"To take to the lawyer. I went to three lawyers before I found one I liked. He couldn't believe I had everything. He wanted to initiate discovery, you know, to find out exactly what he's worth. But I said, 'Don't waste your time. I've got all the records.' And I took him down and opened the trunk of my car. A quarter of a century's worth of tax returns and credit card bills, bank statements. It took me a while to get everything together. I went to the office and took all those records, too. Pam helped me. You remember Pam. We went one morning when he was doing his rounds at the hospital. We just marched in with boxes and emptied all the files. Not the medical records, just the financial ones. They couldn't stop us. When Horace incorporated, he made me a partner."

"Mags." It has gradually dawned on Barbara that some time has passed since the night Mags traced Horace to the apartment. "When was this? When did all this happen?"

"About a month ago, and he's still not really gone. He moved most of his stuff into the garage to get it out of the rain. He took some things with him to the office. He has a shower there, and a couch. He *says* that's where he sleeps. As if I care anymore where he sleeps. But he's always coming around here."

"A month!" Barbara is hurt. "Mags, why didn't you call me?"

"I don't know. You always make me feel it's my fault, and it's not."

"Of course it's not. It's just a very complicated situation."

"Not anymore. It's perfectly simple. I just want him out of here."

"He wants to stay?"

"Are you kidding? He's so dead set against divorce you wouldn't believe it. But I can't go on, Barbara. I just can't do it anymore."

"Of course you can't. You shouldn't have to. No one should have to put up with that."

"But he's begging and pleading, even threatening. He even pulled an ax on me."

"Mags!"

"That night he came home after I threw all his clothes out, I had the deadbolt on and he couldn't get in. He knocked and then started banging on the door, yelling up at the window that if I didn't let him in he would get the ax and break the door down. I'd taken a sleeping pill and it took me a while to wake up. It took me a while to decide whether to open the door. But that door is a hundred and twenty years old and I didn't want it smashed, so I finally went down, and by the time I get there he's gone to the garage for the ax. I open the door and he's standing there with the ax raised over his head. He's holding it with both hands straight over his head, like a madman. I backed into the room, right up against the sofa and fell down on it, and he kept coming. I was sprawled there and he was standing over me with the ax."

"Oh my God! You must have been terrified."

"Oh I was, believe me. I really did think he was going to kill me. But to tell you the truth, at that moment I didn't really care very much whether he did or not. And that helped. But he put the ax down and leaned over me, practically lying on top of me, and he said, 'I would never hurt you.' Can you imagine? After all that, he says, 'I would never hurt you.' I pushed him away. I got up to go back to bed. He called after me. He said, 'I'll be up soon.' 'Will you?' I said. 'Then you'd better bring your ax.' But he never did come up. It took him the rest of the night to pick everything up out of the driveway."

Naturally, after this Barbara worries about her sister—all of the boys are away, moved out, in college or graduate school—and she calls her frequently to see how she's doing. In the course of her conversations with Mags, which are only slightly less bizarre than this first one, Horace comes to seem to Barbara like someone she used to know, a long time ago and not all that well. So she is startled to actually hear Horace's very familiar voice when one day he answers what she has come to think of as her sister's telephone. She's so startled she considers hanging up, but she hates people who do that. Finally she says, simply, "Horace." And he says, "Hi, Barbara." She says that Mags has told her they are divorcing, and he says he doesn't want to talk about that.

"I just want to say I'm sorry," Barbara says. "I'll miss you. We all will. We love you." All true, she realizes as she says it: she will miss Horace; Jack will miss Horace; her children will miss him. "Say hi to Jack for me," he says. "And the kids. Say good-bye." When Barbara hangs up the phone, her hand is shaking.

It's just a few weeks after this that Jack tells her—he comes to her campus office with the plane tickets already in his coat pocket—that Horace, clean-shaven and impeccably dressed, was found that morning hanging from a rafter in the garage that once, a hundred and twenty years ago, was a carriage house, the heavy aluminum stepladder beneath him kicked away with such force that it cracked the windshield of his Jaguar.

AT THE END OF the silver anniversary party, before Horace actually leaves, presumably for the hospital, Barbara and Mags finally get around to telling Jack the story of how Horace once saved their father's life. All was well then, as far as their parents and Horace were concerned. Horace and their father really did enjoy watching football and baseball together, and both parents adored their grandchildren and could not see enough of them. Then their father had a heart attack, and while he was in the hospital—just as Horace and Mags, coming from Chicago, would have been driving in from the airport in their rental car—he suffered a second massive coronary. Horace, arriving in the room as everyone else was standing back from the bed, tore off his jacket, as if preparing for a fight, rolled their father over and whacked his back again and again, hard, with the smooth side of a clipboard he had grabbed from the hands of an amazed intern. Then he rolled their father over again and massaged his heart, putting all his weight behind his hands, like a raging woman kneading bread dough, until their father's heart had no choice but to cry out and live again, for another two years.

A silence falls. Then Horace gets up and takes some keys from his pocket and tosses them to Jack. "Here. Take the Jaguar for a spin."

Jack somewhat resents the condescension, but knows Horace means well, and that he's trying to cover his embarrassment at the story Mags and Barbara have told about him with such feeling, such admiration. Besides, Jack is dying to drive the Jag.

"I'll take Mags's car to the hospital." Horace stands behind Mags's chair again and kisses the top of her head.

"Do you have to go?" Mags says. "We were having such a good time."

"The party's over . . ." Horace sings so tunelessly and off-key that nobody knows where to look. Then, seeing that he's suffered some loss of his customary dignity, he joins his hands together, bows deeply, and says, with a good deal of acquired irony, "Sayonara."

Gregory A. Schirmer

JANE MULLEN grew up in Connecticut but has lived in many parts of the United States as well as in England. For the last dozen years she has lived in Oxford, Mississippi, and for the past six, has divided her time between Mississippi and Ireland. Between them, she and her husband have four children.